Elisabeth Sh
geographical into
transforming Ireland i

of wrath, in which the parenthetical faery tale of the title in part points to the theoretical shenanigans of a certain sort of easy, essentialist, ageist feminism we found in the sixties, seventies, and eighties particularly, and post-structuralism generally. Both prose and thought throughout are ever sparky and surprising, even as they are shot through with a piercing recognition of and negotiation with growing older as a woman in ways that complicate the youthful utopian riot-grrrl clichés—the distance between, say, granny hair worn as a fashion statement by twenty somethings and the bewildering real deal of continuous cellular undoing. The result is ever smart, crisp, astute, revealing, ironic, and richly (sometimes downright brutally) honest, mischievous in form, heart-hammering in its Beckettian comic vision, and impressive in its Nabokovian command over textual and paratextual material shot through with a meticulous knowledge, understanding, and intellectual bite.

Lance Olsen, *My Red Heaven* and *Theories of Forgetting*

Ire Land **confronts the unholy trinity** of gender, violence, and literary representation as Elisabeth Sheffield dares to reveal an ageing female with a deliciously disastrous life in protagonist Sandra Dorn. An unorthodox homage to Samuel Beckett's Molloy reborn as woman, Sandra is a conundrum, unapologetically human, outrageous, and absurd. At a time when society expects her to fall into the cliché of a harmless older woman, Sandra is wonderfully complex, ingeniously flawed, yet so difficult that society doesn't know what to do with her. For these very reasons, she is all the more present for having disappeared. The reader searches for Sandra in emails, in the marginalia of her mysterious editor, in her abandoned children and estranged siblings, and in her cagey colleagues to find a fully complex woman both known and unknowable. Refusing to fall into neatly gendered traps of narrative and linguistic cliché, Ire Land frees the reader from the cultural violence of language with dazzling insight and dark humor.

Aimee Parkison, *Girl Zoo* and *Refrigerated Music for a Gleaming Woman*

***Ire Land* is a formally inventive novel** in which the borders between human and animal, dream and reality and art film might dissolve. A novel that both engages with theory and laughs at its insufficiency. A feminist novel with no patience for sentimental ideas about aging bodies, and a queer novel that casually mutates the idea of queer. Elisabeth Sheffield has given us a novel that takes death and non-being seriously, meaning comically—that allows an aging—disintegrating—human to speak combatively on behalf of her own lived experiences and confusion, the traps she's fallen into, and the desires born from the swamp where biological life meets representation. A brilliant, entertaining, and necessary book.

Stephen Beachy, *Glory Hole* and *boneyard*

In vibrant scene and fearless prose, Elisabeth Sheffield rescues the female body—in its multitude of forms, its metamorphoses, its grotesqueries, its sexualities, its imperfections, and all of its beautiful animal truths—from idealization, idolization, and the tight grasp of those who don't truly see her but write her nonetheless.

Susan Steinberg, *Machine* and *Spectacle*

IRE LAND
(a Faery Tale)

IRE LAND
(a Faery Tale)

Elisabeth Sheffield

SPUYTEN DUYVIL
New York City

Acknowledgments

I would like to thank the following people who all, in one way or another, helped bring this novel into the world: the fair folk of Belfast, Brian Caraher, Libby McEvoy and the late, inimitable Ciaran Carson; the terrific ENGL 5559/"Reading/Writing Ecstasies" crew, especially Katie Woods, Loie Rawding and Ansley Clark; wondrous CU colleagues Katherine Eggert, Stephen Graham Jones, Marcia Douglas and Sue Zemka; former, but still wondrous colleague John Lowney; the amazing upstate curators and creators Marco Breuer and Mina Takahashi; the glorious Stephen Beachy; the kindly but canny Teresa Carmody; the visionary Michael Flatt; the remarkable and ever magnanimous Melanie Sheffield; the smart and dedicated staff of Spuyten Duyvil; and lastly, but not leastly, my beloved, unfailingly supportive, deeply embedded and yet always inspiringly *other*, Jeffrey DeShell.

Additionally, I am grateful to the following institutions for providing funding and support to research this novel: the UK Fulbright Commission, Queen's University Belfast, the Seamus Heaney Centre, the University of Colorado at Boulder and the Hazel Barnes Flat foundation.

The section of Sandra's story following "On Weds, Aug 14th, 2013 at 12:10am, Madmaeve <madmaeve17@gmail> wrote: Have ye no other kin ye can turn to?" was published as "Hare," in *Your Impossible Voice* (Issue 17, Spring 2018).

Library of Congress Cataloging-in-Publication Data

Names: Sheffield, Elisabeth, author.
Title: Ire land : (a faery tale) / Elisabeth Sheffield.
Description: New York City : Spuyten Duyvil, [2021] |
Identifiers: LCCN 2021001593 | ISBN 9781952419331 (paperback)
Classification: LCC PS3619.H4515 I74 2021 | DDC 813/.6--dc23
LC record available at https://lccn.loc.gov/2021001593

FOR LEO AND FRANCIS

I am gone away to the open spaces,
And whither riding no man can tell;
But I shall look upon all your faces
No more in Heaven or Earth or Hell
  —Lord Dunsany, "Fairy Child"

Is anything better, anything better?
Tell us it then:
Us who are old, old and gay,
O so old!
  —W.B. Yeats, "A Faery Song"

McKewan Kambi
4021 204th Street, Unit 1
Queens New York 11361
USA

11 May, 2014

Dear Ms. Kambi:

I am in your mother's room, though it is not I who live
here now. That is for the landlord to decide. In the interim,
I am in your mother's room writing this note. I will leave it
for you, along with a parcel, on top of the press. In regard
to the contents of the parcel, they are mostly a collation
of selected electronic correspondence (both sent and un-
sent) recovered from her laptop, which I cut, pasted and
reorganized—tidied up, so to speak—to provide you with
an account of the last nine months of Sandra Dorn's life, in
her own words. To be sure, I also inserted a few editorial an-
notations of my own, here and there, but only for the sake
of clarification and occasional, ahem, amendment. Then I
transposed the whole digital file into print on paper. For
research has shown that screens and the like interfere with
the intuitive navigation of a text and inhibit the reader from
forming a mental map of the journey (moreover, there are
those perplexing little pixels, which to the human eye appear neither here nor there). One of two hard copies (the
other, along with the digital record, is safe in our archives),
this manuscript is yours to do with what you like. Perhaps
you can pitch it to a publisher. Or pique the interest of a
Boston College scholar—though I am afraid your mammy's
voice comes from a place less credible than the grave. Because while dead men (and women) tell no tales, all human

beings have an intimation of the earth. Terra firma. Yet she is where she is, and this could be considered an account of how she got there. Dear Kew (if I may), I am sorry it is not more.

Sincerely yours,

Malachi McLaughlin
Director of Queer Studies
Queen's University Belfast
Belfast BT7 1NN
Northern Ireland

inista." *Ageism and sexism are old bedfellows, and neither gives a shit about a woman's pleasure...* you wrote in your post the other day about your mum's *pathetic attempt to make [your] da's mickey stand up again with breast implants.* You think you will not serve (though feminista rhymes with barista), you in your hip hugger fatigues and radical fringe trimmed bikini top, shaking your fist at the nubile ideal.

You call yourself a feminista and if you were to read one of my old course syllabi, you'd think I belong to the same camp. The camp that recognizes the essential campiness of femininity, that it's all an out-dated masquerade, *a nostalgic tradition of imposed limitations on women*, as you put it, quoting Susan Brownmiller. Well, you should have seen me last Friday at Conrad and Ormondo's. Speaking of duration's toll, a chin to hold up would've been nice. A chin to hold up, and forget about balls, because the place was already filled with them.

According to Conrad's e-vite, the dress code was "Warhol's Factory" and so I spent too long deliberating between one vintage Marimekko and another—acidic pink and green vs. basic blue and aqua—as if the right color, the perfect shade of cool could neutralize whatever nastiness the night held in store (at the last party, someone had asked if I was Ormondo's mother). Too long calibrating the effect of a pair of black no-lace Converse vs. that of the metallic bronze Arche sandals I'd bought in Paris two years earlier, attending a conference I couldn't afford. With orthotic inserts the sneakers fit like backless bedroom slippers, while the sandals looked like what they were—podiatry in the guise of fashion *pour la femme plus agee*. I decided on the basic blue and aqua shift, with the black no-lace Converse and a fifties beaded clutch, a look that if I were forty years younger would've been very uptown girl on a downtown spree, black slippers and all, but now, when I took one last look in the mirror, announced my impending homelessness. With my bloated torso encased in the too tight vintage Marimekko and my skinny vein corded appendages jutting from the openings, I looked like some horrid George Segal situation sculpture: *Woman who's lost her job just short of retirement and spends her afternoons drinking gin and tonics in the dank refuge of an air-conditioned mid-town bar to escape her rent-controlled studio*. Which is essentially what I am—just swap the unemployment for no savings and the studio for the three thousand square foot reason why. Just before I left the house, I swapped the Converse sneakers for the bronze Arche sandals, the clutch for a classic camera bag.

Old clothes are for the young, lending the funk of experience to those who have none (in America, at least. It's different where you live, where a *trouble*some stink still clings to all, despite the sanitizing effect of *Game of Thrones*). In my twenties, my party outfits were assembled from Goodwill and flea market finds: a Borsalino hat with a *Cat on a Hot Tin Roof* lace slip; a Victorian mourning dress, hiked up at the waist, with rubber hunter's boots, a *Belle de Jour* housecoat with black knee-high men's dress socks and wingtips. Mismatched images from musty cinematic dreams spun from real life. Or was it the other way around—musty real life spun from cinematic dreams? Either way, I reeked of vintage referents, artfully mangled, like a body that can't be identified and so cannot be claimed. Which made them want me all the more: I never went home alone, unless I wanted to.

Back then, by the way, home was the East Village (more or less), and it never took me more than ten minutes to get ready for an evening out; I simply grabbed one of my thrift store ensembles and threw it on. Now, in this Cow Town turned Tech Center where dot.com "style" and utility (sweat wicking, non-wrinkling) prevail, it takes me an hour, and I *always* go home alone. Though to qualify, I'm never unaccompanied—either Conrad or Ormondo walks me to my door, six blocks away, since our arid little corner of Denver is "still in transition." But I suspect it's more for show than protection. How tall, how slim, how *youthful* they look (though Conrad once described himself as his father's last shot in the Battle of Berlin, which would make him my senior by at least two years), guiding grandma home by the elbow.

By the time I arrived, in the old dress that was too young for me, the party had filled Conrad's little xeri-scaped front yard, and beyond—a coterie of shirtless young men in Carhartt overalls (dressed more for the Farm than the Factory, it seemed) had spilled out the low wooden corral of fence (recycled from orange crate slats still stamped with "Sunkist") onto the sidewalk, and now clogged the open gate. I recognized one of them, a thirty year old with a dark chin-strap beard that lengthened the line of his already long jaw, lending him a look of Lincoln-like resolve. At the last party at Conrad and Ormondo's (at least the last party I'd been invited to, six months ago), which had been themed "Semiotics," at the marble topped kitchen island laden with faux Hostess HoHos, Twinkies, DingDongs and Zingers from the new neighborhood French bakery, he'd given me a lecture about the health risks of sugar as I stood licking pink frosting off my fingers. When he noted the *diabetes doughnut* around my middle, I told him that given the context, I liked to think of it as a beignet disguised as a doughnut disguised as a beignet disguised as a doughnut. *Whatever*, he'd responded, then wandered off.

Raising his hand, Chin-Strap parted the cluster of Carhartts, giving me passage but otherwise no sign of recognition. And so on, as I pressed through the crowd to the stacked cube façade of the house, a *Dwell* magazine style dwelling constructed entirely from metal shipping containers (some of which, Ormondo once stage whispered to me, had held human cargo). I was provided berth as I passed a couple dozen faces—digital media and performance artists, hipper species of CU and DU Arts and Sciences faculty (though no one from my own program, Women and Gender Studies), affluent professionals and business people committed to après sport culture, because you can't spend all your time snowboarding, cycling and hiking—berth and nothing more, as if I were a server bearing a tray full of dirty drink glasses back to the kitchen.

One of the faces, looming a foot or so above mine belonged to the agent from whom I'd bought my house. In the past two decades she's transformed herself from the blond Cherry Creek housewife she never was (the last time she'd spoke to me, about five years ago, she told me she was looking for a wife herself) into an ageless Blade

Runner styled (think Daryl Hannah soldered with Rutger Hauer) house-vending machine—"Northwest Denver's top realtor in 2010, 2011 and 2012," according to *Mile High Magazine*. I looked up as I passed by and saw her pale blue eyes slide to the fence perimeter beyond me, perhaps to calculate the square footage.

Inside, I squeezed through the shoals of conversationalists lining the passage between the book-case lined wall and the kitchen island (this time laden with what appeared to be farm to table fare for the artsy fartsy set; I caught a glimpse of a glistening heap of ruby beets flecked with mint, inside a small wooden crate painted to look like an old Brillo box, in homage to both Warhol and Paul Thek), then around the horn of the island to the kitchen counter bar beside the refrigerator. Reaching for the handle of Grey Goose, I felt something brush and scrabble at my ankles. I looked down and Widget, Conrad's shih tzu, met my gaze with a leap, her claws scrabbling at my marimekko. I scooped her up, her red ribboned topknot bobbling as she lapped at my face. At least someone was glad to see me. Securing the little dog in the crook of my arm, I fixed my anesthetic with my free hand: vodka with a tint of cranberry juice. Iceless, in a plastic wine glass, it looked like rosé. Not that I had anything to hide—I'm sure they all assumed I was a lush anyway, if they assumed at all

The far end of the first floor of the house (an open space ten shipping containers long, four shipping containers wide, according to Ormondo) is a sitting area/reading room, situated beyond a low divider of glass vitrines encasing a changing display of artifacts. The last time I visited, there was a tableau of a dozen battling headless rock 'em sock 'em robots, necks exploding with artificial daisies, but these had been replaced by what appeared to be sixties-era, color illustrated travel books depicting some exotic locale—perhaps Ormondo's native Hawaii— the faces of both natives and tourists blotted out with white paper. In any case, it was not the case that drew me, but the attending sense of separation from the rest of the room, the feeling of an isolation tank, which so far none of the other guests had entered. On the far side of the vitrine, beside another bookcase lined wall, shelves filled with Conrad's art, theory and philosophy books, I sank into the cushion basket of his Le Corbusier chair, swinging my metallic bronze sandals (I looked like Mercury without the mobility) up onto the ottoman. Widget circled and settled herself in my lap. As I took a big swallow of pink washed vodka, she blinked.

In Conrad's Corbusier chair, behind the glassy reef of the vitrine, I was, if not invisible to the crowd at the other end of the room, then at least obscured, a distant underwater form, a receding maritime blob of marimekko blues. Even as I knew no one was looking for me, including Conrad, who had surely only invited me out of habit, automated by knee jerk nostalgia for the cutting edge bitch I used to be.

What had I been thinking, accepting Conrad's e-vite? *Old's cool*, you wrote in your last blog, urging your readers to check out a couple of memoirs by *rediscovered* women artists, one of whom is my contemporary, the other a predecessor. Had I been hoping for some kind of riot grrrl revival of my lost self, a carhartt kick start? Old is not cool,

Maeve, or even wise—only old enough to know better. Old enough to know better, I would finish tranquilizing myself in my vitreous cove, and then head home, picking up a refill and a plate of beets on the way out. It would be as if I'd never come. But in the meantime, the leather of the chair cushions was cool and smooth, the foam it covered both firm and yielding. I would leave, knowing better—but not immediately. In truth, at that moment I felt more supported, more sheltered than I have of late in my own home, where creditors and collection agents constantly infiltrate via phones lines and ethernet cables. I leaned back and Widget sighed, dropped her head, making a pillow out of my stomach bulge as she closed her eyes.

Faintly, I could hear voices coming through the open sliding glass doors on the left side of the house. Through the filmy white curtains I could see figures, along with the outline of Conrad's tubular steel octahedron (a gift from a young sculptor friend), on the lawn beyond. The lawn is on a side lot, formerly occupied by a little bungalow, bought up and razed by Conrad, upon the advent of the little old lady owner's removal to assisted living. I'm hoping the grandeur and architectural authenticity (it's a genuine Denver Square, circa 1907) of my own house will preserve it from such a fate. I, on the other hand, possess no saving graces.

Widget snored, the damp circlet of her breath linking with the spheres of the marimekko print. I sipped steadily at the vodka, feeling the slippage of thin fire down my throat, a slight but fervent stream, then a spreading vapor in my chest followed by a slow precipitation, that lightly washed my empty gut before pooling, finally, in my groin. Improbably I felt a pressure, a weight that wasn't just the dog. I closed my eyes and let it sink there, the sensory deception of some long ago head it didn't matter whose or what sort of hair I'd clenched in my fists short plush bristles, long smooth locks, wooly clumps of curls, even none at all just warm shaved skin curved beneath my encouraging palms it didn't matter whose head it was butting my pubis tongue knotting knotting my clit tighter tighter it didn't matter whose head whose head was between my legs.

And then suddenly there was no head no head only the pressure that now and then still mounts but always comes to nothing.

Someone cleared their throat.

I opened my eyes. Ormondo stood before me, Widget tucked under his arm like a reclaimed teddy bear, a pale blue chambray shirt buttoned up to just a notch below his collar bone, displaying the smooth brown column of his neck, the pedestal for his broad boned face and thick, still-dark hair. His broad boned face was in fact even broader than usual, widened and also whitened by what I was clearly meant to take as a welcoming grin. It's a funny thing about teeth: we're supposed to see an exposed set as a sign of receptivity, but really they're just a barrier of bone.

Did you have a nice nap, Sandra?

Then he extended a hand down to me

Editor's Note:
We have left out the quotations in the dialogue, in keeping with your mother's practice in her messages to Madmaeve17. Although their absence sometimes creates confusion in regard to which words are "heard" and which are not (as well as by whom), it does seem to "speak" to Sandra's inability to recognize any external reality outside herself. Does/did anyone else ever exist for her, beyond being a means to fulfilling her own needs and desires? Has she even woken up here? Perhaps she is still napping.

in my chair. If I had the strength, if I were younger, I would've grabbed his hand and jerked him into the book-case behind me, burying us both in a shower of Hegel, Nietzsche and Heidegger. I was that mad—with his phony, bony smile, he'd ruined my reverie.

But I am an old woman (a crone), and he could've just *jerked* back, snapping me to my feet rather than allowing me to contribute at least some measure of the necessary motor force. Further I wasn't entirely certain that I could extricate myself from that chair without struggle. So I extended my own hand, permitting him to take it. The knot in my clit unraveled, my whole body sagged beneath the marimekko print dress as he pulled me up.

Conrad asked me to fetch you, Ormondo said, cupping my elbow.

What could Conrad want with me? Beyond the e-vite, we hadn't communicated in months. Perhaps to use me in some sort of living history presentation, as he had at another party a year or two back, when he'd introduced me as *Taboo-era* to a young pink-haired performance artist: *Sandra here actually saw Leigh Bowery give birth to Nicola Bateman for the first time.* That last bit is true, by the way. I was with Kevin, who after suggested we reenact that nativity at home. He was a lot of fun, my Kev-boy, at least until Belfast took him back.

I looked at the gold antique watch on Ormondo's wrist (his grandfather's, he claimed, though Conrad once told me he'd bought it at an estate sale): it was nearly eight.

Okay, I said. But then I really must flee. Tomorrow's a writing day. Though I knew that as usual, I'd be lying in a torpor until at least noon.

The gauze curtains billowed with the incoming heat as Ormondo slid the glass doors open then guided me over the track onto the narrow cement patio, down a single step onto the lawn, over to the group convened around the octahedron.

The sun was slanting into my eyes (I'd left my sunglasses inside, in my bag on the floor by the Corbusier chair). Squinting, I could see Conrad, standing with a few museum staff people, including the program director and her little boy, who sat in the grass at her feet. Next to Conrad there was another young woman I didn't recognize. She had a long shock of silvery white hair.

Granny hair, I believe your generation calls it. I saw it for the first time in New York a few months ago, during an attempt to see my daughter, Kew (the attempt was unsuccessful, though the flight and hotel charges still went through)—gray tresses on the heads of twenty-year-olds, created by bleach and dye rather than time and travail. It sparkled in the long rays of the setting sun and I thought of glitzy museum dinners, of galas and benefits, of Conrad and Ormondo in tuxedos, with baby-faced, grubby-mitted artists and scenesters in tow. I was invited along once or twice, in another century, but I'm not bitter—the rich are such bores. In fact, I guessed the young woman was some tech industry donor's hip trophy wife, possibly a rising indie actress, with that trendy tinseltown hair.

She slid two fingers along one of the sculpture's horizontal supports: It's brilliant, Connie, just brilliant. You say it's an octahedron? The octahedron is the third in the series of the five Platonic solid shapes, you know. It represents the element of air and is connected to the heart chakra. Love, compassion, beatitude, all that...

Along with the granny hair, she had a granny voice, a cockney granny voice, with a raspy sizzle to it, like the smolder of a lifetime of smoking and council flat bickering... I realized that the woman was decades past twenty, and further, sensed that I once knew her, though when and where, I could not recall.

Conrad saw us, gazing over the tops of his semi-rimless lenses, the frames sunken accent breves beneath his pale eyes. He turned his back and whispered in the woman's ears. She looked up and her features came into focus, but without resolution—I did know her, but still couldn't place her.

Hello Sandra, you sly girl. You never told me you knew Marian Ferris, Conrad chided as they both turned to face me. The woman extended her hand but made no move to come nearer.

I squinted and suddenly I could see her on an asphalt-covered rooftop deep in the bowels of the Bowery, the sun (rising this time, rather than setting) backlighting her dyed black hair (originally a honey brown?) with an aureole of red. Her arms were raised, she was chanting something unintelligible to my ears still ringing from a night of dexedrine and burgundy. Skinny, writhing, she snaked in and out of my vision while I sat rigid, gripping the seat of an old metal desk chair trying to quell the rage in my veins because there'd been someone I don't even remember who, just another bobbing head he (she?) is now, and Marian had fucked him (her?) in someone's shotgun apartment down below. I just know it wasn't Kevin and that the air was thick with heat, so likely it was the summer of 1980.

In the summer of 1980, I was in between lovers. In between lives. Here's a bit of background, for cohesion's sake: back in 1972, on the verge of dropping out of art school, again, a girl walks into a midtown Irish bar and meets a one-legged bartender slash poet from Belfast. It sounds like the beginning of a joke, and it was. But a joke without wit or a punchline, though the blows came regularly enough: my relationship with Kevin Killeen played like a Punch and Judy show, or perhaps Sid and Nancy, as the seventies went on and the bruise of punk rock bloomed, a relentless domestic slap stick kick fuck, with the occasional extramural paramilitary scuffle (as Kevin's old Belfast mates couldn't seem to let him go), for a change of tune. A witless joke, a running joke, a hiding joke, it lasted seven years and spanned two continents (though both Manhattan and Ireland are technically islands), until the day that Kevin died and the farce was finally over.

By the summer of 1980, I was done with Kevin and not yet on with Adom. I'd just gotten back from Belfast and was living in the garden apartment of my older brother and sister-in-law's brownstone, gratis (in sympathy for my losses), in a Brooklyn neighborhood that was **"losses"?** then still more Park Dive than Slope. Not that I minded the low rent, or thanks to fraternal charity, no rent, environs. But there was nothing happening. So when I finished waiting tables each evening in the East Village, rather than taking the F train back "home," I'd head for a bar, a club, cold-water walk-up, or on occasion, uptown penthouse or three-story greystone—wherever the large, loose mélange of musicians, poets, painters, graffiti artists, guerilla girls, chinchilla boys, trustfund punks and well-fixed junkies I then consorted with was gathering.

Marian Ferris was part of this same group—an English performance artist whose act in those days involved the vaginal incubation of blood sausages, which were then externally minced, inserted with toothpicks and served to audience members from a white plastic tray. Marian was against meat, which she described as part of the *global phallocarnacy*, and from the twiggy looks of her, against food in general. But she was not against dicks. This I knew because for a week or so after my return from Belfast, I'd subletted from her roommate, who'd quit the city for the summer with a Quebecoise lover. When Marian wasn't performing, she was mostly fucking, and mostly fucking men, judging by the visitors who passed through her bedroom door.

Twiggy fucking Marian—she was as thin as the last time I'd seen her, on that Bowery roof-top circa 1980, though not as white (back then, then she was the whitest woman I'd ever seen). She was much much browner, as if she'd spent the intervening years in some sun soaked place, but no heavier, in a white linen wrap dress that cinched her waist, bared her arms, tattooed with runic-looking spirals, as black and vivid as if they'd been inked last week, and displayed her smooth bare legs, tattooless, but also unblemished by knots or spider veins, and feet, long and elastic looking in black leather thongs. Each toenail was painted turquoise.

The color matched the narrow eyes that were regarding me regarding her, and at the same time seemed to look past me, as if there was someone else she was trying to see, just a little further on. Perhaps she was trying to reconcile the present with the past, the bloated granny standing before her with the grrrl I used to be. But her hand was still extended, so at last, feeling Conrad's glare, I shuffled over. As soon as I touched her palm, her other hand homed in and covered mine, trapping it. For a long moment she held me there, captured in her grip. Her hands were cool, their pressure indifferent yet unrelenting. It was like some kind of mild trial or maybe an incubation (despite the lack of heat), to force hatch some tiny, stirring feeling. A small but brilliant diamond perched on the forefinger of her right hand, flickering coldly in the waning light.

Hello, Sandy dear, she said in that croaky cockney voice, finally releasing me. It was the only thing about her that was not young. Because even the gray hair, despite the geriatric shade, was anomalously youthful, with its show of supple health. In fact, she looked better than she had thirty odd years ago: the skin that I recalled as subterranean city pale now had a kind of brown prairie glow, which combined with her high cheek bones and squinting agate eyes gave her the mien of a cowgirl seer.

The sun should've been sinking fast—it was well after eight, by now—but seemed to be hanging on, just to hold Marian Ferris in its glow. Again, I wished I had my sunglasses, and not only to shield my eyes from the sun, but from Marian who, no doubt, was taking me taking in the splendor of her resurrection.

I asked her if she still lived in New York. No, it turned out. For twenty years she'd been living on a New Mexico ranch as the *resident artist pet* of an old monied family become new with the scion's investments in the aerospace industry. I recognized the name—they owned storied acreage not far from Taos.

I'm just an old relic, she claimed, sliding the diamond ring back and forth over her finger as she spoke. It sparkled and spritzed, like some miniscule fountain, the bitsy bubbling quintessence of her sexy silver hair. Passed on from one generation to the next, she added.

You mean from father to son? I asked.

Ormondo snickered. Widget dangled from the crook of his arm, blinking.

Conrad raised an eyebrow at Ormondo, creating, with the sunken diacritical of his left lens, a set of parentheses around one chill gray eye: Art is the daughter of freedom, which is not to say that freedom always begets art.

Then Conrad turned his bespoke shirted (crisp white cotton, with blue paisley cuffs) body a degree or two in my direction, just enough to slight Ormondo and reproach me at the same time: Over the course of her *residency*, Marian has produced truly groundbreaking work. That means *not* more of the same, not skillful or not so skillful iterations of museum pieces and corporate collector approved stratagems and techniques.

He paused, shifting his gaze momentarily back to Ormondo. Ormondo's nostrils flared.

Continuing, Conrad addressed only me: Her latest work consists of selfies in which the lens skims so close to the body that it could be said that the subject becomes flesh itself—only it is flesh so out-of-focus that all its identifying features—pores, follicles, hairs, freckles, moles—are completely blurred. It is flesh that is no longer recognizable as flesh. It is an image that is no longer an image. Few contemporary artists have had the courage to so completely liberate themselves from the tyranny of ocular oppression.

Tyranny of ocular oppression, Ormondo repeated. My god, Conrad, what does that even mean? Clamping Widget, who had suddenly begun to wriggle, to his chest with one forearm, he stepped behind Marian, staring over the top of her head at Conrad. The brown column of his neck was suffused with red, as were his ears: Maybe that I should start painting with my eyes closed? Then he walked away, back to the house.

I'm so sorry if I've caused you trouble, Connie. Marian reached out and touched Conrad's arm, her face craning up at him.

Conrad brushed her cheek with two fingertips: Ormo will get over it, darling. Then he twined his hand with hers and guided her away from the rest of us, towards a corner of the yard where stone reclaimed from the foundation of the little bungalow had been used to pave a detached patio, shaded by a white umbrella. I want to hear more about that video you were talking about at dinner last night, he said as they ambled off.

That left me, a twenty-something kid in thin-soled red running shoes (the main cashier at the museum, who always gives me the senior discount, though I've never once asked for it, or even shown my ID), another boy in equally thin-soled yellow ones (one of Conrad's curatorial assistants, I think), and the young woman who organizes the museum's programs and events. I knew her to be the mother of the child sitting in the shade of the octahedron sculpture, bent over an iPhone, his thumbs tapping away. But I've forgotten all their names, if I ever knew them in the first place. At openings, the young woman sometimes smiles encouragingly at me, in a manner that seems to say, *you go, Granny. Gobble up that art!* Though I don't think she has ever actually spoken to me. A slip of a thing with pale taupe skin and a foamy pile of dark hair, she always wears highheeled mules. That night they were silver, and a soaring four inches. Once again I rued my squat Arche sandals. Though of course the real mistake had been coming out at all.

Fortunately no one's attention was on me, as all three gazed over at Conrad seating Marian in the white shaded bower. Idly, I wondered if they were lovers. Not that I cared, but that explained Ormondo's little outburst (uncharacteristic; normally, he is as cool, serene and dull as his paintings). I was about to slip away, when Yellow Shoes said: She's not totally blind, you know—only legally blind.

What's the difference? asked Red Shoes.

I looked it up for my introduction before Conrad's talk about her work tomorrow evening, said Silver Mules. People who are totally blind can't see anything with either eye, while people who are legally blind still have some useable vision. Marian Ferris is only legally blind—she says she can still see dim shapes and movements, as if she's in a dark room. Of course that doesn't make her any less awesome.

Marian Ferris is blind? I asked. The strange way she had looked at me—was the seeming double-vision actually no-vision?

Well, legally blind, Mules said.

Since when?

Since the early eighties, in Belfast. She was helping folks protest against English rule—petitions, pamphlets, posters, sit-ins, slow-downs, walk-outs, rallies, demonstrations, teach-ins, etcetera. So the English threw her in prison, even though she's English herself, or half English—I think her mother might've been born in Ireland. Then she got involved with this IRA guy, something Sands, I think—it's in my notes—and the prison hunger strikes he was organizing. She fasted for 180 days, refusing to take anything but water and when it was over, she was blind. Or almost blind.

I started to say that Marian was in New York in the early nineteen eighties, then realized I wasn't sure. Had I seen her after that Bowery rooftop sunrise? I couldn't (and can't) remember. Further, I was out of the city myself a year or two later—evicted by my brother's wife and living in Syracuse with another brother, an (un)domestic arrangement that led me to seriously reassess my footloose situation, and ultimately, to enroll in graduate school. So it seemed possible that Marian had moved on as well, to new commitments of her own, though it seemed that thinness, both physically and intellectually, still defined her.

And now the twiggy old thing was blind. Or almost blind. What did she see when she looked in the mirror? Dim shapes and movements? It would be like being underwater, and yet I was (am) the one who's drowning. I hadn't thought about Marian Ferris in years and years, and here she was, rescued from oblivion, dripping with late career success, silvery hair a sparkle in a sun that refused to set. It hurt my eyes.

Mommy, Tway's hungry.

It was Mules' son, and "Tway" was evidently himself,

there being no other referent. He was still sitting in the grass. The iPhone lay abandoned by his little lime green fishermen's sandals. His hair was in neat twists, like Kew's, before she shaved them all off, his skin a taupe similar to his mother's. He looked a little like Kew at the same age, though with a slickness to him she never had, his shins and knees without a scrape or a scratch, as if he'd been raised on a set or a film studio. An image of Kew suddenly came unbidden, screaming out of the dark at someone's party in the mountains that she was being chased by a ghost, or maybe it was the host's tow headed son, her spindly limbs flapping, head a halo of twists bobbing on the stalk of her neck like some freakish woodland flower. I must've been stoned.

Okay, Trey, let's go inside and get something to eat. Mules held out her hand and he leapt up and grabbed it, nearly toppling her. She recovered, laughed: Hey you, what are you trying to do, take down your own mom?

Red Shoes reached over and swept the kid up by the armpits, swung him around in a circle, then flipped him, gripping him by his ankles. Dangling, squealing, his twists falling like an upside down crown, the kid's face darkened with his own young blood. Red Shoes carried him off. His mother and Yellow followed, neither even looking in my direction as they went.

There's no exit through the high wooden fence that surrounds Conrad and Ormondo's side yard. In this neighborhood, an exit would also be an entrance, inviting graffiti on the interior as well as the exterior of the palings (Conrad, despite his patronage of "street art," abhors the work of our anonymous local artists). There was no way out, but at least the sun had finally dropped. In the gathering dark, I could see the white clad forms of Conrad and Marian Ferris beneath the white umbrella, in the stone-paved corner of the lawn, and I could hear the murmur of their voices, but not what they were talking about. I'm sure they didn't even know I was still there. And in the meantime, my stomach was empty, gastric juices gurgling, as if I were having a conversation with myself. Inside, there was a kitchen island covered with communal fare, to which I had as much a right as anyone. I'd fill my belly (I'd had nothing but a half tub of expired hummus all day), replenish my vodka, and leave, as I'd planned to do a half hour ago.

Someone had put on what sounded like electronic tango music. I could see forms in the conversation area beyond the vitrines, but the space around the kitchen island had largely cleared. A group stood at the other end, near the front door—Yellow Shoes was there, plus a couple of young guys with beards, a girl in a button down, short shorts and an enormous pair of pink framed glasses, and a sixty-something man with a flop of gray hair and a Moroccan vest who looked like the actor Jeremy Irons and who had his arm around a twenty-something boy. The boy looked like Jeremy Iron's son. The girl held court for the males, her hands shaping the air into voluptuous curves as she spoke. She was inaudible over the music.

Only a handful of the ruby beets remained in the Brillo box. With a toothpick I speared them, and put them on a paper cocktail plate. There was a shallow black ceramic bowl with a few stubs of sliced peach mixed with nibs of crytallized ginger, though the centerpiece, an intact peach fitted with a blond Barbie torso, evoking the buttocks of a Yuskavage nude, had survived. I took that, too. For protein, I snagged the last of the cheese from the wooden cheese board—a wedge of asiago. There were no crackers left, but in the shade of a vase of green spider mums, on another cocktail plate, I discovered a trio of glistening chocolate truffles, each topped with a coffee bean. Someone's take home treat—why shouldn't it be mine? I'd eat my beets, my peach, my cheese, washed down with more vodka. Then I'd scoop up those three little chocolate tits on my way out.

This time I drank the Grey Goose straight—no blush of cranberry for me. I had nothing to apologize for as I stood with my back against the bookcase lined wall, stuffing my mouth with sweetly acrid beet, then swallowing it down with vodka. If anyone dared to approach me, if anyone tried to start a conversation, I'd bare my red-stained teeth, then honk in their face. Fuck Conrad, fuck Ormondo, fuck Marian Ferris. Soon the beets, then the cheese, and lastly, the pear, were gone.

I closed my eyes, took another mouthful of vodka. I swished it around in my mouth, swallowed, took another gulp, exulting in the burn. The music changed. Now it was some sort of techno hip hop, though a saxophone sounded in the background of the beat, like a senile bray from someone else's hipster past. Certainly not mine. I might honk, but I never would bray.

When I opened my eyes, Conrad's dining table, a modernist slab of solid teak, had been pushed to the side, and in the tiled expanse between the open kitchen and the vitrines, people were dancing.

One of the dancers was Mules, who having cast of her shoes, had become Barefoot. Trey, who really should've been home in bed, and a tall young man, whom I recognized as my old pal Chin-Strap, were dancing with her. All three were doing a kind of shifty twisty thing with their feet, a bouncy side to side sliding movement that enlisted frisky hips, at times breaking into a backwards forwards shuffle that gave the illusion of being on a treadmill. Of going nowhere, but so quickly, so fluidly that despite my dislike for the music, I found my own feet moving in response, and for several long seconds it was all I could do to resist the tide of their dance, not to mention the undertow of vodka. I only managed to stop myself by imagining the hospital bill that would follow if I fell. I still have insurance, but the deductible is obscene.

Something flashed white on the bottoms of Barefoot's feet. Gripping my drink (almost gone), I moved closer. It was surgical tape, on the balls and heels. To make her slide better, I assumed. I marveled: she'd prepared in advance, to dance. She probably had a retirement account as well, annuity funds prudently distributed among stocks, bonds and real estate. So that thirty or forty years from now, she'd still be dancing. And in the meantime, she had a fine sheen on her forehead, and her foamy hair shimmered and shook beneath Conrad's murano glass chandelier. Chinstrap's eyes were on her, as he duplicated her shifty, twisty, hippy sliding with his own, but hers were on Trey.

The kid was an even better dancer than his mother, his feet, now in lime green socks, flitting and capering over the floorboards, his tiny pelvis clad in matching lime striped shorts orbiting his strong little trunk, his stripling arms waving, his fingers curling then unfurling, as if he were scattering enchantment about the room. Oh he was magical, just magical I tell you. I wanted to puke. And then suddenly I not only wanted to, but had to. I rushed to the bathroom, which fortunately is just off Conrad's kitchen, at the bottom of a stairwell behind the book-lined wall.

Editor's Note: Unlikely. But he does sound like an appealing little fellow, just the same.

Beets, cheese, pear—it came out in layers, with the beets on the bottom. A toilet bowl parfait. I looked in the mirror. Something I once said to my mother came to mind. I must've been about eight or nine and she'd found a drawing I'd done of her in her goliath brassiere and girdle: *You don't have to get all huffy and puffy about it.* Swimming in the mirror was a blowfish, swollen with self-loathing.

Editor's Note:
Poor Dolores ("Dolly") Dorn (nee Peplinski). According to one of our informants (a first cousin who still resides in Canton, NY), your Grammy Dolly in her youth, before she met that "mean mick bastard out in Colorado," was "slim and pretty as Kate Hepburn in *Sea of Grass.*" In fact it seems the dairyman's daughter, beguiled by Hollywood images of life on the high plains, once aspired to be a cattleman's wife, and went west to seek her fortune. No need to comment further on the outcome of that venture, but it is worth noting that your mother's own early trajectory in the opposite direction, from Colorado to NYC, was equally ill-fated, and further, in the end only landed her back in the region she despised.

I steadied myself on the basin. My arms shook. A drop of water clung to the faucet, like snot to a nostril. Then I heard voices outside the door. I waited for a twist of the knob or a knock, but neither came.

Are you sure you'll be alright?

No worries, Connie. Now that I'm an old woman, I've got whiskers. I'll feel my way.

I'd say it sounds like altitude sickness, but as I recall, Taos is even higher up than here.

Tis only a wee bit of lightheadedness. I just need to be horizontal for ten or fifteen minutes in your lovely guest bedroom, then I'll be back down. Why don't you go check on poor Sandy?

Ah, yes. Poor Sandra...

She used to be magnetic, you know. Truly magnetic. And so talented and clever. While I would not have predicted academia for her, I'm surprised to hear she hasn't gotten on better.

Even now, she can be amusing. But she's been her own greatest foe, every step of the way.

Every step of the way. I listened to Marian's feet, girl light, barely audible ascending the stairs. Conrad had presumably returned to his party, in search of me, or more likely, in avoidance. I felt a hotness on my throat. I looked again in the mirror: a hive had risen on my neck, a swelling much smaller than my blowfish visage, but also genuinely toxic. Or potentially so. As Conrad had just put it, I was my own greatest foe. If the hive grew any larger, or got any deeper, it could constrict my windpipe. At one point, I was prescribed with an epipen. But that was back when I had a better health plan. These days I rely on benadryl and over-the-counter zyrtec. I thought of my camera bag beneath the Le Corbusier chair, then remembered I'd switched bags just before I left the house. Had I transferred my pills? Probably not. When I was younger, I wouldn't have been caught dead carrying a purse, and now I would be, though technically the purse was under the chair.

Again I heard someone outside the bathroom door, then another tread, much heavier than Marian's, or even Conrad's, going up the stairs. I opened the door.

Ormondo is allergic to finned fish. Years ago, at a sushi restaurant, there was a mishap with some yellowtail. I still remember his smooth olive face going scarlet—I attributed the shade to rage. He was just back from visiting his parents in Hawaii, and Conrad and I had had a fling in his absence. As it turned out, Ormondo's immune cells were more suspicious than he. He never had a clue.

I'd guessed right that it was Ormondo on the stairs. The dog was no longer under his arm. I pointed to the hive on my throat. He whisked me up to the master bedroom, through to the attached bath, where he pushed me down onto the edge of the tub, pulled an epipen from the medicine cabinet, peeled off its sterile wrapper, and injected the syringe into my thigh. My lungs opened and I took a deep breath. Beneath the disinfectant gleam of tile, there was an odor of old urine.

Lifting me up by the elbows, he led me back into the bedroom, sat me down on the queen-size bed, then took a seat beside me. The bed faces a wall that is almost entirely windows. The lights of downtown Denver winked in the dusk.

After my father left her, my *makuahine* had a hard time. She'd always been so vibrant, the life of the *luau*. But then she sort of just deflated, let herself go...

I looked around the room. Although the lights were off and the sun had finally set, there was still plenty of illumination from outside—the glow of street lamps, porches, windows, the glitter of downtown beyond. The room looked exactly as I remembered it from fifteen years ago, clean, modernist, serene, with two of Ormondo's paintings (which as long as I'd known Conrad and Ormondo, have never hung downstairs), male nudes, on the walls.

In daylight, you would be able to see the warmth in the gray tones, the abalone shell/pearlescent complexity of the monotone palette. I knew Ormondo was trying to be kind. Conrad once told me that he couldn't paint for six months after his mother died. On the other hand, no man (or woman) had left me, at least not recently. I wondered what he thought my excuse was. Did he know about my house? I hadn't (still haven't) said a thing about it to either him or Conrad.

Ormondo put his big hand over mine. It was cool, and soft. I smelled something faintly sour, fermented, like yoghurt. The scent was not unpleasant. In the ambient dim, I could see his feet on the floor, long and veiny in a pair of old birkenstocks. Take your time, he said. When you come down, I'll walk you home.

He left the room. Music pulsed up the stairwell. A white sheepskin rug lay on the floor at one end of the wall of windows. From the rug's matted appearance, I assumed it was where Widget sunbathed. I also assumed that at night she shared the queen-sized bed, as her predecessor, Iggie, had during my sleepover all those years ago. Perhaps they'd let me have the sheepskin, and I could sleep there in the corner, on the floor. Mornings I could clean, scrub away the scent of old men's piss. But of course I couldn't stay. I couldn't stay, anymore than I could get the bank to refinance my house. All the credit I had ever possessed was gone. If I left now, maybe I could at least avoid seeing Marian Ferris on my way out. As far as I knew, she was still resting in the guest bedroom down the hall.

Downstairs, the music was changing again. I stepped out of the stairwell into a dry, rapid drumbeat, a ripping baseline, the metallic roar of a harmonizer, the disco rasp of Freddy Mercury and machine guns ready to go. Was I ready? Was I ready for this? Not any more, though years ago I could jump and dive for dust as lustily as anyone on the floor. They were all out there now: Barefoot and Trey, Chinstrap, Yellow Shoes and Red, Pink Glasses, Jeremy Irons and Son, the Carhartt Coterie, the House Vending Machine, Ormondo, even Conrad, who had seized Ormondo's hand with his own, and punched the air with their conjoined fists, rhythmic as a piston, two synchronized hearts throbbing as one. It was as if their spat out on the lawn had never happened.

And then Chinstrap was lifting little Trey up above his head, probably in a bid for Barefoot's attention, but the gesture only served to further elevate the boy, who writhed ecstatically beneath the murano glass chandelier. He reared up, arched his back, shook his twists, diving into the arms of an awaiting Carhartt, who then passed him on to Red Shoes, and so on, so that he appeared to dip and swoop over the dance floor like a tiny, grinning godhead. Hosanna, hey sanna, sanna, sanna, hosanna, hey sanna, hosanna hey, around and around he went, buoyantly bobbing on the small sea of outstretched arms, passing from one set to the next, including Ormondo's, including Conrad's, as if he'd never grow old, as if he'd never die, as if he'd never bite the dust. I couldn't stand him.

I simply couldn't stand him, even though he looked like my daughter Kew once did, or maybe because he looked like my daughter Kew once did, only better. Better, well cared for and tended, with his freshly done twists

41

and little lime striped shorts, like an advertisement for Swedish designed children's clothing, or a poster boy for the health benefits of eating more fruits and vegetables. He looked like a reproach. A reproach who was now sleepily regarding me from over his mother's shoulder, his legs hugging her torso. Barefoot had pulled him from dance floor, and stood with him by the food, her back to me. He smiled, then frowned a little when I didn't smile back. He shifted in his mother's arms, his head sinking below her shoulder so that I could no longer see his face

I looked up and saw Conrad coming toward me, Ormondo behind him, once again toting Widget. No doubt it was to hustle me out with an exit cue disguised as a goodbye. Would Conrad let me retrieve my purse from beneath the chair, or would he send Ormondo to retrieve it for me? But then they gathered on either side of Barefoot, both men leaning in to pat and smile at Trey: You are a marvel, Conrad pronounced.

I am not a marble! But I am on youtube! the kid replied in an unnecessarily squeaky voice. They all laughed.

Barefoot hoisted him up her hip, tousled his twists with her black painted nails: I better get this little guy home—he's got art camp tomorrow.

Don't forget those tweats, Mama, he squeaked again. His mouth was smeared with viscous brown, like lipstick applied by a drunken hand.

Here, let me get you a container for those, so they don't get squashed. Ormondo circled to the other side of the island, and began rummaging in a cabinet above the kitchen counter.

I reserved a table at Linger for after the opening tomorrow. If your au pair is still away, young Mr. Youtube is welcome to join us, Conrad said, reaching out again to run a benedictory knuckle over Trey's forehead.

The kid pressed his palm against Conrad's: I want YOU to carry me to the car.

You can't just tell people you want them to carry you, Barefoot reprimanded.

Why not? Everyone needs a little support, now and then. Conrad lifted the brat from his mother. He squirmed a little in Conrad's arms, nuzzling laundered cotton as he made himself cozy. Finally he settled, with his face tucked into Conrad's left armpit.

Okay, this should work, Ormondo said, returning with an empty Greek yoghurt container.

Oh, thanks so much. Barefoot took the container and reached for the chocolates sitting in the shadow of the spider mums. My three little tits—though now there were only two. She snapped down the lid. These are for tomorrow, Trey. We can each have one.

Trey lifted his head: Why can't I have both? There was a sticky looking brown smear on the shoulder of Conrad's shirt, where his mouth had just brushed. I knew that if Conrad even noticed, he wouldn't care. Years ago, he used to let Kew maul him without protest, to snatch off his glasses, nibble at his eyelashes, explore his nostrils with her baby fingers. And back then it amused me to watch— to see cool Conrad turn all warm and fuzzy, diacriticals dissolved.

I knew that if Conrad even noticed the smear, he wouldn't care, so why did I have to point it out? Why, with trembling finger raised, did I have to say what I did,

43

a stream of invective that I think began with *look what you did to his shirt you spoiled little shitty mouthed squeak toy* and ended, as his eyes grew wide and his mouth opened but no sound came out even as his lips quivered and his small jaw shook and ended with something like *come on let it rip you greedy dipshit let it go you youtube dancing boobie come on come on I want to hear you bellow like the colossal brat you are you should've been in bed hours ago.*

Someone had turned off the music, and the only sound in the room was my own ragged breath. It felt as if something had torn in my chest, had wrested free and now was flapping around the room on bile-slicked wings. Maybe I was having a heart attack. Maybe Conrad's aghast expression, Ormondo's look of mortified concern, were countenance to my cardiac arrest, and nothing more. Maybe the inconceivable vitriol I'd just spewed was just that—some private cranial chimera generated by the thoracic event below. Maybe I'd said nothing, maybe I'd simply turned some sickening hue, clutched my chest, knees buckling, as I now felt them beginning to do, while the shelves of the bookcase behind me ratcheted down my spine. Maybe they were all staring at me because I was straddling the tile floor, marimekko hiked up by my bloated belly, skinny legs askew.

I think she's melting, said Pink Glasses.

Let's hope so, said Chin Strap. He put his arm around Barefoot, steering her after Conrad, who with Trey clasped to his chest, was headed out the door.

I think it was Ormondo who guided me back to the reading area beyond the vitrines, and lowered me into the

44

Corbusier chair, while Conrad called a taxi service (Sandra being in *no condition to walk home alone, unfortunately*). There was no direct light source as it was now dark, and the lamps remained off—only the reproachful glow of the kitchen down at the other end of the house. Again, I leaned back and I guess I must've dozed a little because I didn't see Marian come into the room. In fact, I'm not sure she came in at all. It might have been a dream or at least partially a dream. Certainly there was no conscious explanation for the odor of cold stone and earth opening in the dry heat like the entrance to a cave as I felt someone kneel beside me and murmur in my ear, Och, ye poor craythur. Nor for the voice which sounded like Marian's croak only the accent had shifted west, across the Irish Sea, and north, to somewhere far up in Ulster. My da's country. But surely as I cracked my lids it was Marian I saw before me holding an earthenware mug. Agate eyes gleaming, the little jewel on her forefinger glittering in the dim as she leaned in, urging me to take it: Tis only water, darlin'.

Only water, cold and pure—clearly not from the Denver municipal tap, but from some more essential, spring-fed source, or at least from a well-chilled bottle (She'd gotten it from Conrad's private stash, I guessed. I remembered a minibar in his study upstairs, though I hadn't been in there in years). I gulped the water down, realizing as I did how dry and sore my throat was, stripped by the drinking, the vomiting and finally, the ranting. Relief came almost at once, and as my eyes involuntarily filled with tears, I closed them. Saline leaked down over my cheek though I wasn't crying, god no, it was way too late for that, and the smell of stone, now dampened as if with moss, grew stronger. And then I felt some small hard edge slide up over the curve of my cheekbone, a fingernail maybe, tracing the path of moisture, heard a croaky voice whisper *Sláinte*, followed by what sounded like a slurp.

So that was five days ago, my dear Maeve17—five irreversible days following one irreversible night. In some parallel universe or alternate dimension perhaps another Sandra Dorn exists who is not a mortgage defaulting, child assaulting (though contrary to the claim of Barefoot's attorney, there was no physical component), hate speeching (if only the boy had been a towhead) hag—but instead a home-owning, heart-chakra opening, unicef giving grandmother of eight. Another Sandra Dorn, who, say, began toting a purse in junior high, stuffed with kotex pads and kleenex packs, life savers and doublemint gum, dog treats and teething biscuits, change that was for bums but could be mad money, too, just in case. A good girl who carried not just a purse, but a shopping list, who knew not only what she needed but also what she could afford, never made impulse purchases, mishandled the merchandise or got kicked out of the store for discourteous or incorrect behavior. Oh, I've been *bad*, I admit it, and now I've reached a place where there are no returns. After certain incidents, there is no going back. Not enough years remain to undo what's been done, to unsay what's been said. At my age, there is no temporal wiggle room in which to assemble a *new household out of friends*, as you wrote in your post last week, after you left home *to get away from [your] begetters' heterosexist bull shite.*

Conrad and Ormondo were the last of my intimates, in fact ceased to be years ago—though the Platonic ideal of friendship remained, a decorative structure of courtesy that was in its way comforting. If I had actually had a heart attack or a stroke the other night, they would've rushed me to the hospital. And if the heart attack had been just a heart attack, unaccompanied by that little scene, they would've brought flowers and clandestine Widget kisses to enliven my convalescence. Conrad and Ormondo were the last of my intimates, and I won't find any others. I have lost every means—looks, charm, money, professional influence, not to mention a domicile—necessary to collect a new household of friends, at least the salaried, credit holding kind (though I suppose if I were to remain in this city, I would eventually find a new circle beneath the I-25 underpass).

Barring the underpass, I am afraid my last resort is family. Not my da, or my fat old ma (who at least, I now realize, retained a waistline), both of whom are long dead, nor my grudge-bearing Brooklyn brother and his wife. But the Syracuse one (unmarried) still has a soft spot for me, and my little sister in Lake Serene, whose affections I've hardly tested, has reached out (she heard of my "situation" from Brooklyn, who I must confess I wrote first. I could stand Park Slope now that it's grown so much hipper, but it seems they still can't stand me.) I just received a message from Irene yesterday, offering her "guest cabin." Yes Irene of Lake Serene. If that sounds like too much, it is. But what other choice do I have?

So wish me luck, MadMaeve17. And please do keep writing those feisty, idealistic posts—they make me feel young again, and capable of seizing the world by the balls. In fact, if I could get a grip again, I would rip them right off (to replace the ones I have lost, despite my claim above).

On Tues, August 13th, 2013 at 12:10am, Madmaeve <madmaeve17@gmail> wrote:
I wish I could help.

It has been two months since I last checked email and I just found your message, Madmaeve. I wish you could help too—more than ever. Lend your strong young arms to getting me out of here. Though there's nothing I can't manage to carry, or rather drag—just a rolling duffle packed with chicos tunics and no tummy pants in earth tones (think sand, pebble, rock, paper, scissors, shoot) of cotton modal, rayon, nylon, acetate and elastane (a.k.a. e-z care travel fabrics for the woman whose body has left her taste behind, or no more marimekkos for me), pharms and toiletries (benadryl, zyrtec, contact lens solution, medicated Tucks), a few copies of my books (like I could even give them away), the last laptop I got from the university (which technically I should've returned, but fuck 'em), a couple of packs of emergency smokes. Sure I've got baggage, but that's not the problem.

Early yesterday morning Irene told me that I don't have to go. I was sitting on the porch steps of her cabin, since the guest cabin steps were still sticky with syrup, smoking and slapping at mosquitos. I'd been up all night. Just me and the owl hooting softly in the pines: *whooo whooo. Whooo whooo do you think you are?* The screen door creaked behind me and I felt cool fingers on my shoulder: *You can stay Sandy, if you want.* She stepped by me, nightshirt brushing my arm, trailing a scent of clean cotton and unwashed crotch.

She strode away towards the woodshed, her white shirt lit through by the low sun sweeping across the lake. I could see the long lean line of her naked back, straight as a boy hero's. Shoulders to depend on. She could save me still. Even though, I realize now, she's probably always hated me. Our da wanted nothing to do with her. When she would wrangle for some outdoorsy invitation (to go fishin! Or huntin!) I'd already declined, he'd tell her to leave him alone: *Get yer butt ugly face out of here. Butt ugly:* that just came into my head, though he never used the term with me. I wonder what that was like, the denigration—good preparation for old age, maybe. Then again, as yesterday morning's sunrise made transparently clear, now she's the favored one, by Father Time if not Father Dorn.

According to her, it's *all the work.* All those goddamn chores, *better than Under Armour,* she insists. Especially woodcutting. I watched her balance a log on its end on the chopping block, then reach for the ax leaning against the shed door. All the job did for me is turn the inside to meat jelly as well as the out. Tenderized by lactic acid and black

50

fly bites, quivering for the cleaver. I felt like an accident waiting to happen the whole time I was there. An accident that maybe she will help me to make happen, if I go back.

Irene raised her ax. *Swoosssh... Thwack.* Did she imagine each log was my head? She tossed the split wood to the side, reached for another log from the pile. *Swoosssh... Thwack.* Or did I imagine it was hers? Either way, the head count was not good. I decided to row across the lake and walk into town, before I lost mine, again.

That is where I am now, more or less, as I write this. Not in the eponymous hamlet across Lake Serene, but in another larger community twenty minutes south that calls itself a "village." No longer rowing and walking distance, but not so far that I can't say I just needed a day to think things over. I might even be able to get Beryl or Darryl or whatever the name was snoring in the corner over there to drive me back. I'll paddle across the lake myself.

A week or two ago, Irene told a story about stumbling upon a hibernating bear. How she had noticed a tendril of steam rising up *like cigarette smoke* from a balsam mounded by snow, how her snowshoe caved through the roof of what turned out to be a kind of pine branch supported igloo, at the bottom of which a snow dappled black bear lay curled, fast asleep. *I backed away as quietly as I could,* she said. *Then I hightailed it out of there. You don't want to mess with a bear.* Maybe she now feels the same about me, wonders if she should've unobtrusively slipped away when I emerged from the passenger exit at Albany Airport, instead of driving the bear one hundred and sixty miles north to her home.

Although she actually never had a chance since I saw her first, and would not have let her get away. I was desperate. Am desperate, all the disparagement above notwithstanding. I recognized her instantly, though I hadn't seen her for fifteen years. Her blond kinky hair (*like a head of pubes*, as our dear da described it) had gone gray but the rest of her was the same as the thirty year old photo on the back of her *Woodchick* books, tomboy lean body in a red and black buffalo plaid flannel tucked into a pair of harness leather belted levis, bunched a bit about the waist, girlnextdoor tanned face. The same and yet not the same, as I saw a couple of punkalicious Asian kids in pink hair and combat boots abruptly stop, turn and click furtive photos of her.

I withdrew behind a pillar, regarded her scanning the faces of arriving travelers, thumbs hooked on her belt, legs akimbo, rocking a little on the heels of her workboots. Back then she'd looked the little woman, a skinny cutie trussed up in hubby's weekend slobwear to help with the camp chars. But now there was something deliberate in her appearance, bunching and all, a new millennial hipness, a timberland cool, that was neither wood chick nor wood dick. It was as if she'd escaped the binary, the sartorial pitfalls of both sides, and was standing sure-footedly in the shifting territory of the third sex, that elusive fashion space rarely reached by anyone over thirty five, and then only by certain musicians and the occasional resurrected nineties poet or conceptual artist. Now her plastic rimmed owl-eye glasses—the same frame she wore back in the eighties—looked like an aesthetically informed choice, rather than a vision plan necessity. Now

Editor's Note:
No spectacles were
found amongst your
mother's effects, despite
her myopia. It can
be assumed that she
eschewed the styles pro-
vided by her own vision
plan, and elected to wear
contact lenses instead.
But contact lenses can-
not be worn constantly
(especially by the elderly,
who frequently suffer
from "dry eye"), and thus
there is some question
here about acuity, along
with accuracy.

her leathery brown skin was the single batch success of a cultivated nonchalance.

I rued my chicos ensemble. What was I thinking when I charged all those horrible clothes to my visa card? That the earth tones would signify my willingness to try an earthier lifestyle? Nevertheless I stepped out from behind my pillar and waved: Irene! What choice did I have? She turned, stared blankly in my direction, then took me in. I felt her assess and attempt to place my beige and gray bulk in some other corporate colored terrain besides the airport—the bank, the insurance agency, the dentist's office. Perhaps I'd helped her get a better policy for her four by four truck.

Or maybe she did recognize me, but was giving herself time to process my transformation. Either way, she compensated for the lag, if there had been one, with a preemptive hug, clamping me in a woodsmoke scented vice. Then she stepped back: You're going to feel so much better, once we get some balsamifers into those lungs.

I nodded agreeably, though I had no idea what she was talking about.

As we walked to the baggage area, she explained that the needles of the mountain pines *tanged* the air with *airborne medicinals.* That nineteenth century doctors had called these *balsamifers*, and that they had once made the Adirondacks a vast sanatorium for tuberculosis patients. I wondered if she thought my problem was as simple as a disease of the lungs, a mere physical malaise that had made me no longer fit to cope. Testing this hypothesis, I gave a consumptive little cough as I reached for my duffle bag on the baggage conveyor belt. Instantly, Irene swooped in, lifting it out of my hands and hoisting it over her shoulder, despite the back saving rollers on the bottom.

Outside, a four by four did indeed await, though no simple utility vehicle this—at least not anymore. A Willys jeep truck like our da once drove (but unlike his, without a scratch or ding), a matte red brown, in cold blood cool. The color could've been rust but also, given the evenness of its texture, paint that merely mimicked the look of honest oxidation. Either way, it was to die for, just like the twenty something femme fatale inside the open windowed cab, strong sensuous features shadowed by a plain black baseball cap, torpedo boobs barely contained by a white tank top, smooth shapely arms, braceleted at the biceps with snake tattoos, resting on the steering wheel. A hipster wet dream though I suffered no illusions myself as she touched a finger to the brim of her hat. It was the barest acknowledgment of my presence at the passenger door, which she made no move to open, while Irene secured my duffle under a tarp in the bed in back.

Irene opened the door on the driver's side and got in, the young woman scooting over. Hooking her arm around the woman's neck, Irene smiled through the cab at me, still standing out on the curb: Sandy, this is Kristal. This beautiful thing came up to me after a guest lecture I gave at her university two years ago and I've been smitten with her ever since.

I saw a flash of white teeth beneath the black brim, a snippet of pink tongue as Irene leaned in for a long kiss. When it was over, the girl turned to me, adjusting her cap as if to straighten the veil of shadow over her face. Nice to meet you, Ma'am, she said. Then she reached over and pulled the latch on the passenger side door.

I should not have been surprised, given Irene's new millennial makeover, but still I marveled, much as she probably wondered over the change in me. At any rate, it was a quiet four hour drive north, all three of us in the one seat of the cab, with Irene at the wheel, Kristal now seated in the middle, and me riding shotgun, my shoulder pressed against the door, trying to keep my eyes on the dark wall of trees whizzing by on the side of the Northway. The last time I had seen Irene, back in the early nineties, she was living with Ted or maybe Todd, a wild life biologist or ecologist whose research had been something incredibly small and obscure—something like the biomass of insects as opposed to plant matter in the pygmy shrew diet. So dry she had seemed, with her crinkly hair, beef jerky skin and washed out blue eyes. So awkward and stiff with the need to prove her girlish grit in territory always already marked by the boys, as during dinner she'd gone on about what it had taken to be one of the few women certified as "a bonafide Adirondack Guide," while Ted or Todd stood with his back to us, poking at an early summer fire in the woodstove. I'd felt my own ovaries shrivel when she attempted to shift from monologue to dialogue, asking what I thought of eco-feminism, and if I'd read Françoise d'Eaubonne (whose name she pronounced as "Fran-soyce Dough-bone"), and had avoided her the rest of the evening by reading a huge chunk of Harry Potter to Kew, then turning in early with a headache.

But now, as the air slipping through the driver's side window vent tousled her gray blond dreds, as the beautiful girl leaning into her shoulder murmured unintelligibly in her ear, I could not stop looking at her. How I wanted to drink whatever she was drinking, whatever had made her so vividly fluid, so fluidly vivid. I tried to find something else to look at, but even the roiling purple cloud mass moving in on my right was like some indie cinematographer's big fucking symbol for Irene's newfound midlife passion.

The rain held off until we reached the camp (I won't detail the motorboat glide over the jade waters of Lake Serene, which was just another scene in the sundance fantasy of my sister's senescent success, a fantasy in which it felt like she was both main actor and director, and in which my own part was invalid if not obsolete). But just as we docked, raindrops began to dimple the lake. Lightening flashed white through the dark branches of the pines followed a few seconds later by a crack of thunder. Irene hustled me up onto the wooden deck, once more hoisting my duffle over her shoulder, while Kristal stayed behind to tie up the boat and tarp it over.

Canopied by white pines and hemlocks, Irene's guest cabin is a dim place, even with its big picture window facing the lake. At dusk under a storm darkened sky it was practically a cave, illuminated only by an oil lantern which Irene lit as we entered. So I did not see the beetles that first night. What I saw was a flickering fantasy space of timber and tinsel, a log walled Adirondack jewel box filled with shelves of leather bound books and antique colored glass, killims and gleaming animal pelts, brass-riveted vintage trunks and iridescent feathered fishing lures. The last hung from the rafters, so that they hovered just over our heads, like a flock of mutant hummingbirds. Best of all was the big brass bed in the corner, heaped with pillows and trapper's blankets, a silver beaded dreamcatcher affixed to the log wall over the headboard.

I expressed amazement, only partly feigned.

Built it myself, out of forty five virgin spruce logs, cut in midwinter when the sap was down and the bark tight to the trunk, Irene drawled, dropping my duffle on a trunk at the foot of the bed. I lived and wrote here for sixteen years, until last year, when Kristal came up for good and we built the new cabin and writing studio.

I tested the mattress with my hand. It felt like a featherbed laid over a firm futon. It's perfect. Thank you.

She moved over to the little table in front of the picture window, straddled a spindle back chair: You know I owe all this to you, Sis, in a way. That time you left Kew with us and took off for two weeks. You never really said what you'd been doing at your conference, or whatever it was, but by the time you came back, me and Todd were done. We'd been talking about having a kid. But after just a few days, no way. Boy or girl, it would've only made things worse.

Lightening dazzled the windowpanes, thunder split the air. She was silent for a few moments, a dark silhouette against the dark again glass. When she resumed, the rain was coming down so hard that at first I wasn't sure I was hearing her right:

And you smelled. You stunk like you'd been in bed for a week, and not alone. I wanted to stink like that too. Or not. I wanted that freedom, to fuck someone for days on end, or to just be alone with myself. So I built this place, and when I wasn't fucking, I was writing my books. It was great, and now I've got Kristal.

Wow, I said, sinking down into the bed.

Hey, I didn't mean that like it sounded. Her teeth flashed white through the gloom. I always thought you were the coolest. I still do. You were a trailblazer for me. I left Colorado because you did. We all did. I don't know exactly how things went wrong for you—seems like you should've been set with the professor gig and all, even if it was back out west. I still don't have that. But I want to help you. I want to help you get back on your feet.

I now lay stretched out on the bed, which didn't, by the way, smell like sex. It smelled like wool and lavender, it smelled like a well cared for old lady. I closed my eyes.

Before she left, she came over and stroked my cheek. Then she muttered something. I couldn't hear her over the thrumming on the roof, but through half-closed eyes saw her point to a mason jar on the bedside table. I guessed it was supposed to be my chamber pot, since there didn't seem to be a bathroom.

I didn't fall asleep immediately. Gusts of rain were

Editor's Note:
"We" meaning your mother's two brothers, Steven and Johnny, as well as Irene. All three looked up to the firstborn Dorn, at least early on. By the time you were born, your mother, according to Steven's wife Karen, had become "a pain in the neck." Yet all three of Sandra's siblings acknowledged your birth with cards and gifts. Steven, as executor of Steven Sr. and Dolly's estate even tried to set up a trust for you. She was still their kin and by extension, so were you. Kin: a word beyond our ken.

58

blowing against the screen of the window above the bed, spraying my skin and bringing in the odors of wet forest dirt and pine—balsamifers.

I woke up the next morning to bird song and the thwacking rhythm of what sounded like wood chopping. Sunlight streamed through the picture window. Telling it slant but true: this was a sweet deal, this rustic rentfree cabin. Maybe I'd even start writing again, at that little table with its view of the lake. Not the academic crap, or even another quasi-memoir, but poetry, like before I met Kevin (having quit after; there wasn't enough room for two bad poets in the family). And maybe I'd try drawing and painting again, too, arboreally inspired abstractions say, or sculpting scavenged woodland debris, like back in the Alphabet City days, when everybody was dabbling in something, mixing it up, mixed genre, mixed gender, mixed taste, when if you were young and pretty, you didn't have to choose.

I needed to urinate but not as badly as usual even though I hadn't gotten up once—not even to undress. I could not remember the last time I had slept through the night, even when I still had my sleeping pill prescription. That I hadn't woken up with a pressure in my bladder and a hollow in my belly, necessitating a trip to the bathroom and then to the kitchen. Last night's dinner had been nothing but the smallish pizza slices Kristal had grabbed for us from a road-side bar while Irene pumped gas into the Willys. But I wasn't hungry at all. Maybe I'd shed a few pounds up here, as it looked like there was no place to store or fix food, beyond the woodstove set into the back wall of the cabin. And tighten up my urethral muscles as well, since I sure as hell wasn't going to piss in a jar. I'd save it for the outhouse, wherever that was. Kevin came to mind again, Kevin and the two-room cold water flat we shared that winter in Belfast. The merely mild discomfort of the trip out the door and down the hall to the WC—a discomfort that was mitigated by or mixed with the pleasure of returning to bed. When I didn't have to choose, even though I was already pregnant for the first time. At least not for the first month or so...

Languidly I rolled over, half expecting to see Kevin, his black hair fanned over the pillow, his long, grub white back. But of course the space between me and the wall was empty. I fixed on the rough texture of the logs. *Bark tight to the trunk.* That would explain why it was still on. It looked like skin, gray scabby skin, but it wasn't ugly. I thought that Irene had been right to leave it, to forego naked logs. Like skin it softened the hard shapes beneath.

And then something moved. A shiny, blue black as Kevin's hair, inch long twitching shifting something emerging from a whorl of gray bark. Pulling the blankets up around my neck in case the thing fell, or flew, I leaned forward a little, squinting. What I saw was not just one insect but two—hinged at the abdomens. The black carapace of the top one split open and with a whir of tiny white wings it lifted itself and its companion into the air, disappearing somewhere amongst the fishing lures above. Suddenly I saw them everywhere, mostly coupled but also a few solo, whizzing across the cabin, arcing up into the rafters, dropping towards the floor, alighting on the bookcases, crawling across the picture window, traversing the trapper blankets, beading the dreamcatcher overhead with shiny black as well as silver, with living, lurching cabochons.

Shaking, I slid out from under the covers, lowered my feet to the floor. First came a prickle then a crunch beneath the ball of my right foot. I think that must've been when I screamed because by the time I got outside, Irene was there, ax in hand. But not to help. She knew what I had been "yelping" about, the "spruce beetles," and reprimanded me for not using "the killing jar" she'd left on the bedside table, before I went to sleep, like she had told me to. Then she went back to her chopping, leaving me to the swarm of black flies that had descended the moment I opened the screen door.

A half hour later, breakfasting at the new cabin (almond flour skillet flapjacks cooked by Kristal over the woodstove), I noticed that the log walls were bark stripped and varnished smooth. When I commented, Irene said, we all learn from our mistakes, don't we?

Still I tried, Madmaeve. And so, I have to admit, did Irene, though I soon learned that her promised "help" required much labor on my part. The great chunks of time I imagined that first morning, to think and to create, were gobbled up by daily assigned chores—chores that Irene claimed would strengthen both my body and my mind. Instead of writing poems, I fetched water from the lake with metal pails (no plumbing), instead of painting canvases, I split logs for the woodstove (no electricity). Cleaning in particular sucked up a good part of the durée. The daily sweeping of both cabins for mouse droppings and in

61

the case of my own, the dead spruce beetles and sawdust borings as well. Washing dishes and washing clothes—each task required not only water but heat, which in turn entailed more wood for the stove. And then there was the sheer tedium and toil—the lifting, the toting, the hefting, the whacking, the hacking, the stacking, the scrubbing, the rubbing, the brushing, the wringing, the hoisting, the hanging, the dusting, the sweeping. Even now, just writing that last sentence, I feel like keeling (over).

And that wasn't all. Because as much time as these quotidian chores ate up, they didn't consume the entire day. With three of us, we easily finished them by early afternoon. With two, the two being Irene and Kristal who worked tirelessly together, like newly wed lumberjacks, like love yoked timberbeasts, they probably could've been done even sooner. But there were other jobs as well—matters of seasonal upkeep, of maintenance and repair, restoration and preservation, many of which seemed to involve the application of caustic liquids to various wood surfaces and the inhalation of noxious fumes. Since Irene wrote in the afternoons, she delegated these to Kristal and me (how the noxious fumes were supposed to work in relation to the curative balsamifers was unclear). She also, it turned out, wrote in the mornings, but since her mornings began well before mine, the full details of her schedule initially escaped my notice.

Evenings brought the labor of conversation, of me enduring them enduring me over epoch paleo repasts prepared by Irene. Each item on the menu bore the burden of backstory: the smoked bear meat came from a yearling treed by a friend's huskie dog, shot down by Irene;

the pickled fiddleheads had been gathered in spring by Kristal, who'd used a traditional Iroquois method to preserve them; the grain in the salad was spelt, a species of wheat cultivated since 5,000 BC; the wild raspberries were the gift of a summertime lakeshore resident recovering from a chainsaw accident, whose aid Irene had raced to in her speedboat after hearing his screams from a quarter mile away, etc. And when the food lore ran out, the animal tales continued—of bears and beavers and otters, of bats and flying squirrels, of wrens and warblers and myriad other avian whatchamacallits (Kristal was a "birder"), the wilderness equivalent of people talking about their pets, the fallback chitchat of dull dinner companions everywhere.

No longer, I noticed, did Irene attempt to engage me in intellectual exchange, about ecofeminism or the like, even though I learned, from fetching the mail each morning (it was delivered by boat, and constituted the main source of contact with the outside world since there was no internet, and only spotty cell service, which is why you haven't heard from me in almost two months, Madmaeve), that she carried on an extensive correspondence with feminist environmentalists. In fact, on the two occasions that our table talk deviated from food and animals, it was Kristal who initiated the shift: the first time to ask what I

Editor's Note:
Your mother notices that Irene does not attempt to engage her in academic talk, but does not speculate why. Although the subject was never broached during your mother's residence with her sister, it is safe to say that Irene knew how Sandra lost her job as a professor of women's studies, and steered clear of all talk related to the profession in order not to embarrass her. Since you were already estranged from your mother and a thousand miles away when the story broke out, you may not have heard about it (though it received national coverage). A full report of the incident, which involved classroom nudity and sexual role playing, can be found here: www.westword.com/2012/12/colorado-professor-forced-to-retire-over-prostitution-lecture-in-feminist studies-course

thought, *as a former professor of women's studies, about top surgery?* (a conversation Irene quickly squelched, saying *it's better not to get some things off your chest*); the second to inquire if I'd read Barbara Walker's *The Crone*. Apparently, the book had been on the syllabus for a course she'd taken *on feminist reclamations of ancient and aboriginal myth*. This topic I killed, saying no, I'd been dancing with the wolves when it came out.

But I tried, I really did try. And around the fourth week, things got better. The spruce beetles retreated back into their holes and the black flies abated. Sure the mosquitos picked up the slack even as my muscles never hardened, but there was a kind of high in that subcutaneous mix of venom and incapacity, a gelatinous yet spikey feeling, like being drunk on jello shots of my own flesh. And then there was Kristal... Kristal, my fellow postmeridian drudge during the hours that Irene wrote. Toiling beside her beneath the hot July sun was another form of intoxicant, one that as the days went by, seemed to reel us both out, leading to conversations and confidences that never happened in the morning or in the evening, when Irene was there.

Yes, things got better, which only made them worse.

The turning point came about three weeks ago, on the third day of an assignment to paint every wood surface that touched soil or water with a nasty at first preservative that turned nice, tar smell mingling with the salty sweet of Kristal sweating beside me, as the afternoons stretched on. Creosote, I think it was called. I wish I had a bit as an olfactory keepsake, even now. We'd finished both sets of cabin posts, foundation logs and porch steps, and had moved down to the lake to treat the dock timbers. Between us stood the gallon can of caustic fluid, as we lay stretched out over the warm deck on our bellies, painting the sideboards and pilings, down to where the water lapped the wood. Now and then, dipping my brush, I'd steal a glance at Kristal, at the long line of her back broken only by the strings of her black halter top, at the crack of her ass visible just above the waistband of her khakis, the dividing line between what I guessed to be two perfect hemispheres of flesh. Lucky Irene. Oh so lucky, only six years younger than I and yet so blessed with nubile plentitude, Irene. I thought about how I hadn't a young lover for years. How for years I hadn't had a lover at all. (Really. Last night was my first fuck in almost a decade).

A smallish fish with yellow and black dorsal stripes swam through the green water below and I found my mind drifting back to a woman I slept with, off and on, back in the early eighties. Jane or Joan—I don't remember which it was, though I remember the name of the bistro where she waitressed: *Jean's.* I'd wait for her to finish her shift around midnight and then we'd go back to her apartment or mine, depending on whether or not she felt like taking the F train out to Puke Slope. Jane or Joan, I can't even picture her face though I can see the shape of her head the black at the roots blond shagged hair covering the neck touching between the shoulder blades of a back that was a bit fleshy across the top but then deliciously bony down the center, rib flutes divided by a beaded strand of spine flanked at the tail end by two dimples, springboards to the magnificent mounds of her ass.

Backs and asses—my two favorite body parts. Parts

of the self that the self can never fully see, and then only with the mediation of a mirror. I would cover Jane or Joan's with kisses from her shoulders to the creases where her buttocks met the backs of her thighs as she squirmed and sighed beneath me, marking every inch of a territory that was already mine, well before the moment I finally staked my fingers in her cunt. But in the end she'd turn around, face me with that face I can't remember, and suddenly I wouldn't want her at all. Always, that is where it has ended for me, with women, but also with men as well. The failure of desire. Maybe if I'd wanted more, I wouldn't be where I am now. I looked down again at the lake water, but the fish was gone.

So when Kristal broke the silence, resuming a conversation we'd started late in the afternoon on the previous day, I was in a more cynical mood than I might have been otherwise. Or maybe it was the beetles, still scuttling at the back of my mind. We'd been talking about Kristal's youth on a reservation in Onondaga County (or was it Oneida?) in upstate New York, about gender roles in tribal culture, and her earliest memories of being attracted to other girls. Just as she'd started on an account of her *first time with a woman*, in the women's locker room (surprise surprise) with the mother of her putative boyfriend (of course), as said boyfriend, a star ice hockey player, was scoring for the home team, Irene had called us to dinner. Today, she finished the story, postgame IHOP pancakes and all, a tale that I won't bother to recount here, as we've all heard about if not tasted the LGBTQ variations of amorous indoctrination. Familiar, too, is the discourse that now followed, on having sex with women versus having sex with men. But as that bears upon what came next, I'll recount it here.

With women I feel whole, not different, Kristal claimed. The brim of her black baseball cap masked her face in shadow: she looked like no one and everyone. Setting down her brush, she sat up, grasped one hand with the other, and stretched her snake banded arms first above her head, then behind her back. Her breasts seemed to inflate her halter top, stretching the fabric taut. The word "bazooka" came to mind, not the gun, but a name on a bubblegum wrapper. They were all that kept her from being seriously beautiful. Or beautifully serious. I thought about the way I'd seen Irene put her arm around Kristal's shoulders, draped hand casually grazing, and I guessed that she wasn't too concerned with Kristal's intellectual attributes. And I also thought about how Irene was no more deserving of her than me—my sister just preferred the ventral side of the fish, while I was more interested in the dorsal.

But you *are* different—you're always different, I said. A dragonfly spun metalloid blue out of the sky above her head, then shot off over the lake. Identity is a fiction: Gender Studies 101, I added. I couldn't resist.

She pulled her knees up in front of her chest, wrapping her arms around them: I mean that with women I feel truer, I feel more secure.

I looked at the snakes encircling her biceps and wondered what they meant to her. I thought of Medusa. I thought of the python's hug. Sounds of brittle snapping and crunching filled the hush. The other day Irene, going over *the specs* for the dock job, had identified the source of the sounds: otters dining on fish bones. But now Irene was up in her studio, writing her book, corresponding with her eco-feminist colleagues, some as far away, going on the postmarks, as Papua New Guinea. There was a plop, two plops, three as a trio of cat-sized heads glided out from the reeds along the shore, then submerged to the slaughter.

I wonder what Irene would do if you had 'top surgery'? I dipped my brush in the can, flattened my bulk against the deck and started painting again along the sideboards, filling my nose with creosote.

For several minutes she didn't answer. The lake water lapped the pilings, the hot planks pressed my breasts and belly and I felt a seal of sweat form between skin and wood. I lifted my torso a little and there was a little squelching sound. If she didn't respond, I wouldn't press her. She was happy with Irene and I was just a spoiler.

Then she spoke: My mom left the res when I was two years old. Dad was a SCAB a stupid Caucasian American bastard she met at a bar or maybe a buck in the woods. I mean no one really knew the man. Grandparents dead from the usual whitepeople diseases. I was raised by my mother's first cousin, who already had four kids of her own. So things were tight, you know? I got everything there was to get for free—government food, church donated clothes, ten-mile bus rides to the county school. When my high school science teacher told me to apply to Cornell because they had a Native American recruitment program, I went for it. Cornell gave me the full deal—tuition, room, board, even a little monthly stipend. I decided to double major in Native American Studies and

Environmental Science, and academically I did great. But outside of class it was weird. All these white valedictorian dykes from their high property tax funded high schools. Even the brown girls were white. They all said how cool it was that I grew up on a reservation. And of course everyone wanted to fuck me. Some of them even invited me home for Thanksgiving Dinner. But it was always like we wouldn't be eating this corn if it wasn't for you—this fake reverence. So yeah, what I said earlier about feeling 'whole, not different' with women—that was bullshit and you called it.

I put my brush down, pulled myself up on one elbow and looked at her. Maybe she was looking back at me beneath the brim of her cap—I couldn't tell. Reaching behind her back with both hands, she undid the halter top, which tumbled down into her lap. Unbound, her breasts were not ridiculous. But they weren't serious either. In their smooth dense globularity they just *were*—organic shapes without meaning or character. The nipples were dark brown, flaccid in the heat.

She stood up, unzipped her khaki shorts, and let them fall to the deck. Then she stepped over to me, leaned down so that one breast pressed my arm and for a moment I couldn't even think, as if the weight was pushing against my brain as well as my arm. I smelled her sweat mixed with sunscreen but it was just a smell, without source or sense. I saw her dark eyes but I couldn't even remember, for a second or two, what eyes were for. She got up with a snort and throwing her cap to the deck, dove off the edge of the dock.

She swam out fifty yards or so, slicing the swells with

a strong freestyle, then she circled back and around, coming within a few feet of the edge of the dock. Treading water, panting a little, she said, But it's not bullshit with Irene. I could see, below the surface, the pale fluctuation of her body.

And now I was furious. How dare she oppress me with her ungraspable substance, with her supple and slippery zeal? But this time I didn't lose it, like I did with little Trey. Instead I moved to the edge of the dock, swung my legs over and let the cool lake lick my feet. She stayed where she was, water slicked head bobbing, gazing at me defiantly, like a child or an animal, like I had some power over *her*.

At the other end of Irene's wooden trestle table, where the three of us dined together, there is a varying stack of books and manuscripts, review copies from colleagues and publishers that come with the daily mail. Every day, after lunch, I'd see Irene carry two or three with her to her writing studio. But one slim, dust surfaced manuscript always stayed, never shifting from its place beneath an unwashed coffee cup printed with the words *Mama Bear*. I've memorized the title page: <u>Earth Medicine: Native American Ecofeminist Strategies for Healing the Planet</u>, *an Honors Thesis submitted by Kristal Shenandoah in partial fulfillment for a Bachelors of Arts Degree in Native American Studies Program with a Minor in Environmental Science. Cornell University, May 11th, 2013.*

Then why hasn't she read your thesis? I asked. Why isn't she helping you edit and revise it? Why, instead of helping you get into graduate school, does she have you doing mindless labor all day while she sits in her studio, writing?

With the word "writing," she disappeared. And for several seconds I could see only ripples, as she'd sunk out of sight. She shot to the surface again just to the side of my dangling feet, her mouth full of water, which she spat up at my face.

But over the next week it became clear that my barbs had sunk into Kristal's baccalaureate degreed brain. At mealtimes, she no longer went with Irene's flow of foodie lore and animal palaver. Now she wanted to talk about books, things she'd read in college, or more topically, the books and manuscripts that regularly arrived in the mail, and temporarily resided on the dining room table, before reaching the sanctum of Irene's writing studio. And while I never heard her attempt to bring up the subject of her own dust accumulating manuscript, the subject of top surgery resurfaced over breakfast one morning.

That morning, I'd arrived at their cottage, as usual, with the mail, which it was my assigned task to collect from the 9:30am mail boat (and which obliged me to set the alarm for 9:25—just enough time to roll out of bed into my chicos and hustle down to the dock). But unlike every other morning since my arrival, no hale smells of cast iron cookery drifted through the screen door. Inside, there was only Irene, who informed me that Kristal had gone for a walk in the woods. Would I please fry up some grub while she finished writing a review? Well, there's nothing that ruins my appetite more than food preparation (I owe my bloat to take out). But I did the best I could with the plastic baggies and jars of co-op whatnot that I found in the larder.

Half an hour later, we all sat in our customary places, Irene at the head, opposite the pile of books and manuscripts at the other end of the table, Kristal (who'd just walked in the door) to her right, and I to her left, plates of hapless flapjacks before us. I gazed down at my own gray and greasy stack. Eating at that moment was more daunting than cooking had ever been.

So I was glad of the distraction when Kristal began reading bits of a letter from a Cornell classmate who'd had her breasts excised, and was now, after an extended and painful recovery, enjoying her unbound chest and *the sensation of warm wind through my t-shirt*. The friend described the surgery as *a graduation gift* from her parents, who'd conceded, finally, to the argument that it would help her tennis serve. Though apparently they had agreed only to breast reduction, not breast removal, and had been upset when she came home for a visit looking, as she put it in the letter, *just like my brother*.

No, I bet she looks worse than her brother, Irene commented, dribbling syrup over her flapjacks.

Kristal stuffed the letter back in its envelope: It's not about how she looks, it's about how she feels.

Well then what she feels must be self-hatred. Sounds to me like a clear case of internalized misogyny, Irene pronounced, cutting into the stack. She pointed a glistening gray forkful at me: What's your take, Sandy?

The question surprised me. What year was it the last time she'd wanted my "take"? 1992? I wondered if she'd somehow witnessed that strange encounter with Kristal on the dock the previous week. Or maybe Kristal had told her about it. Irene was staring at me, eyes widening slightly. I stared back. Then she stuffed the flapjack loaded fork into her mouth.

I looked across at Kristal, who had pushed her plate aside and was now reaching towards the other end of the table for a book. Then I improvised on a French theorist that I was certain that Irene, despite her apparent popularity on the college lecture circuit, had never read: *Flying anuses, speeding vaginas, vanishing breasts: there is no castration.*

Irene sprang up. For a moment I thought she was going to hit me. But instead she went for the metal food waste pail by the wood stove. With her back to us, she hawked. Then she picked up her plate from the table and scraped the rest of her breakfast into the trash.

Yuck, she said, resuming her seat. That almond flour must have gone bad. She leaned back, rocking the chair a little, her hands braced on the tabletop. Veins wormed beneath the skin. Christ Sandy, did you even bother to check?

Kristal put her book face down, folded her arms across her chest. I noted the title: *An Eco-Warriorwoman's Life Journey.* I sipped my coffee. Irene looked old this morning—livid and despite the almond flour stand, whipped. I thought I'd heard voices in the night, though no actual words had carried over to my cottage. As Kristal got up and began to clear the table, my sister stood as well. Walking around to the other end of the table, she gathered up the books and mail privileged for delivery to her writing studio, including Kristal's manuscript.

The next morning, when I went out to wait for the mail boat, I found Kristal sitting cross-legged at the end of the dock, hunched over her cellphone. I knew, from a technically successful though otherwise futile attempt to communicate with Conrad and Ormondo a few weeks back via my own cell, that the dock was the only place it was possible to pick up a signal. I sat down a few feet away. Kristal tapped at her screen and the lake water lapped the pilings. The air held a lingering chill, despite the sun overhead, and a scent of something fishy. An orange monarch butterfly flitted over the dark waves, discretely alarmist. I wondered what Kristal was texting, and to whom. Somewhere along the lakeshore, a woodpecker banged at a tree while another bird I couldn't identify filled the space between whacks with its liquid whistle. It could've been a code, an arboreal SOS. Send Out Succor. Perhaps the mastectomied former classmate would offer deliverance. I could see the girl, could see a whole team of beautiful boy-chested girls, driving north in someone's mother's old Volvo, to save Kristal from that old slave driving Adiron-dyke. Ha. In my mind's eye I made an orgy of Irene's grief.

Fifty shades of schadenfreude scattered moments later by the roar of an outboard motor. Kristal pocketed her phone and I gathered up a sack of mail from the mailwoman.

Up at the big cabin, skillet corn bread crusted with melted parmesan sat atop the woodstove, fresh blue and white checked cloth napkins marked the three place settings. Irene motioned us to our seats. I saw her stroke Kristal's cheek as she brought the corn bread to the table, then watched Kristal lean into the caress, and understood that domestic accord had been restored. Indeed, I then learned that the mysterious texting on the dock had been prompted by a shared matinal experience. Corn bread in hand, Irene explained how they'd been *lolling* in bed together when *a bird serenade* began in the balsam outside the bedroom window. Well Kristal identified the source as an Eastern Whoopdeedoo or some such, which apparently was remarkable in our woodland environs (my attention flitted away for several moments here) and had gone outside to text news of the birdy anomaly to a friend at the Cornell Ornithology Lab.

And now, Irene announced, wrapping up the last piece of corn bread for me in a sheet of wax paper, to take back to my cabin, we would all *relax* for the rest of the morning. In the afternoon, we'd hike out to *the beaver dam*. I could expect a knock on my door around three.

I committed the sin of omission, Madmaeve, when I listed the contents of my duffle bag. Zipped into a little pocket of the lining, I have a stash of old friends, stockpiled during my years on the university pharmaceutical plan (if only I could've shown the same foresight with my retirement plan, and doubled my monthly contribution like the TIAA-CREF quarterly board letters always advised). Most of them are past their expiration dates, but so am I, and when things become particularly difficult, together we get along well enough. I've in fact enlisted their aid several times these last two months, to help withstand the agitations of life on Lake Serene. Back at my cabin, I swallowed two, then picked up a murder mystery I'd found on a shelf tucked between a scholarly investigation of the legend of Sacajawea and an encyclopedia of Adirondack flora and fauna. *Mountain Mayhem: Inspector*

Malachi Tracks a Female ADK Serial Killer. I spent the next several hours floating on a sanguine stream of gratuitous violence, languidly following the detective's blood sequined peekaboo game with the survivalist femme fatale, and finished shortly before three. Just enough time to ingest another two pills, and fill a canteen with one of the half pints of gin (so discretely portable) I'd picked up during our last expedition into the village, mixed with a splash of lacustrine aqua. Details which are neither here nor there but then again may help explain how I later so completely lost my bearings, Madmaeve.

Irene's hat may have played a part as well. Red felt, fedora style with a little black feather stuck in the band, it was, she claimed, the traditional headwear of the Adirondack guide. Single file, Kristal in her black baseball cap, and I bareheaded (though my hennaed wisps probably could've used the coverage) followed it through boulder strewn forest gloom tricked out with moss pelted logs, stray roots and leaf rot masked sinkholes, at last emerging into a too bright meadow where hair snagging pines and mosquitos gave way to bushes, brambles, and stinging deerflies (black fly season thankfully past) and finally, countless bruises, scrapes, scratches and welts later, to a slight slope with a surely impenetrable wall of wetland weeds at its base, beyond which lay what was either a small lake or a large pond, but either way appeared dull as ditchwater. My impulse, when Irene nevertheless strode on, parting the swampy, chest-high thicket with her well-protected arms (both she and Kristal were wearing long sleeved flannel shirts, jeans and duck boots; I'll leave my own attire to your imagination), was to snatch that fucking hat of her head and send it sailing over the bulrushes.

Instead, I calmed myself with a swallow from my canteen, and followed. A few squelching steps later (if you're envisioning my footwear as permeable, it was) we were on the other side, gazing at an expanse of black water, pustulated with yellow lilies.

There, Irene pointed.

What? There was nothing to be seen but water and more vegetal matter. I turned my attention to a mosquito feeding on my forearm. Had it fed on one of the others first, or was the blood threaded with insect parts mine alone?

I see it, Kristal said. She was spraying her hands, neck and hairline, the only areas of her body exposed to the air, with citrusy smelling repellant. But it seems abandoned.

I looked again in the direction that Irene had pointed. A big heap of dead branches, and trunks, what appeared to be old storm debris, the random wreckage of some long past weather event, jutted out of the shallows about thirty yards down to our left. A patch of grass grew out of the top. Just past it, there was another pile, this one longer and lower, which could've been shoreline debris, only water glimmered beyond it—an auxiliary pond or maybe a stream.

Irene nodded: Yep, they've moved on. Looks like they're still around someplace, though. See those fresh birch branches over there? She gestured toward some white sticks floating in the water off to our right.

By now I'd figured out that "they" were beavers. And the two brainless heaps of arboreal rubbish were their ar-

Editor's Note:
The *dobhran losleath-an*, or "broad-tailed otter," was revered by the ancient Celts for its wood working abilities and family values. Hunted to extinction by the 16th century, it is slowly being reintroduced to the UK through wild life management programs in the north of England, Scotland and Wales. Though not in Northern Ireland, where the Troubles have hindered environmentalist efforts. Tis a pity, for this kindly craytur would be a mollifying influence, to be sure.

chitectural efforts. Or, as Irene went on to explain, the *lodge* that had served as their living quarters, and the dam that had created *a viable habitat*, for foraging. Once, she said, a mating pair and their numerous offspring had occupied the lodge, but the last time she had hiked over here, just before Kristal moved in, there'd been only a single beaver lumbering along a stretch of shore stripped of edible wood: *the old female*.

I'd seen enough. But unfortunately, my satiety with the sights was not shared. Irene and her red hat plunged on, taking the shoreline in the direction of the floating white sticks, leaving no option but to march, or squish along behind her, first straight and then along a cattail lined curve where the shore bulged out into the lake—a sort of peninsula or promontory, it turned out. Frogs croaked and plopped, insects buzzed and hummed. Irene simply droned, going on about the wondrous ways of beavers—about how the females, which grew as large or larger than the males, were *equal partners*, about how *mature adults mated for life*, about how they devoted themselves to their *kits*, which they worked with tireless industry to feed and shelter, about how they resolved all disputes without violence or acrimony. Kristal was mostly silent—spellbound I presumed by my sister's little fur family tales. I stopped, unscrewed the cap of my canteen and took a swig. Then stopped again. And again. So that rounding the end of the promontory, I lost sight (and sound) of the other two. When I finally caught up on the other side, they were sitting, shoulder to shoulder and apparently whispering together, on a boulder that rose up out of the reeds like a throne, facing an inlet thickly fringed with ferns, tall grasses and sapling trees.

As I approached, the whispering stopped. Irene turned, a finger pressed to her lips.

There was no room up on the boulder for a third, even if they had attempted to accommodate me, which they did not. But next to it there was another rock, slab shaped, which at least provided a platform above the shoreline mire. I could've sat on it, like a child at their feet, but instead I stood, leaning against the side of the boulder, and looked out at the water. My legs were shaking.

Like before, I saw nothing at first but black water and vegetation, but then Irene reached down and tapped my shoulder, directing me with her index finger to a movement in the bracken about twenty yards to the left. A tree trunk emerged, plowing out from the shore, then swerving round in our direction, propelled by a sleek brown head. As the head drew closer, I could see big orange teeth glaring in the late afternoon sun like an organismic example of bad taste (I've always thought the beauty of the natural world is overrated). Gliding past us the animal continued with the floating tree to a glade of reeds, in the center of which stood a heap of sticks, which I took, based on the earlier sighting of the abandoned *lodge*, for its nest. Presumably there was a dam someplace too (not that I gave one).

The beaver dove and for a few minutes the tree trunk bobbed unattended on the surface.

Check out those incisors, Irene whispered. They never stop growing. If beavers weren't constantly chewing, their teeth would become a handicap. It's the same with anything in nature. Everything has its purpose and if you don't use it, it turns into a liability.

On the other side of Irene, Kristal slid off the boulder, splashing a little in the water. To my surprise, she came round and stepped up next to me on the slab. I smelled the citrus bug repellant, along with an undercurrent of sweat seeping through the additional barrier of flannel. I imagined the bicep encircling snakes beneath, moist and hot. Had Kristal elected to wear the long sleeved shirt on her own, or had Irene suggested it?

And suddenly, I thought of Kew. When I'd picked her up from Irene and Todd's, her arms had been covered with impetigo, the precipitating black fly bites (and looking back, I realize it must've been the height of the season) so thick that, as the pediatrician back in Denver put it, it had been *a field day for streptococci*. In my mind's eye, I recalled the moist golden crust of the infection on her skin—like cornflakes. Or parmesan topped cornbread. Irene could've taken better care of her, but then again, so could I.

And then the beaver surfaced again, followed by five others. One its own size and four much smaller, but all with great glistening no doubt growing before our very eyes orange incisors which, lining up, one large and two small beavers on each side, like picnickers at a picnic table, they proceeded to sink into the wood. I could hear their crunching from thirty feet away, as Kristal, inexplicably, leaned into me, pushing my other shoulder up against the boulder. I looked up, but Irene was staring at the beavers, rapt, and so I took in the press of Kristal's flesh. But what I felt in turn wasn't what I'd felt on the dock. Or rather, this time I could still think. And what I thought of was Kew. I missed her. Miss her.

What happened next is a bit of a blur. I suppose Irene must've glanced down for a moment and seen her girl-friend leaning into me. Something brushed the top of my head and then I saw Irene's arm in front of my face, her hand reaching for Kristal. I shifted back, and either before or after I lost my balance the beavers slapped their tails on the water and disappeared but regardless the sound mixed with my own pratfall into the muck. And now I was on my back in a bed of reeds, Irene looking down on me with her arm around Kristal's waist, her face fulsome with concern. Kristal gazed off, abrogated by the brim of her cap, like none of this had anything to do with her. *Are you okay*, Irene might have asked, or *let's call it a day*, I don't remember or couldn't hear, as if the slap of the bea-vers' tails was still sounding in my ears.

But somehow I managed to pull myself up and then stumbling around the rocks into the lake found the wa-ter surprisingly welcoming, a relief even, smoothing over irritations, cutaneous and otherwise. So I kept on going, splashing out past my knees, past my hips, but still only up to my armpits when I reached the tree trunk, bob-bing in the water. I grasped it, attempted to hoist myself, sopping chicos and all, up over the slippery bark surface, imagined sinking my weak teeth into it, banging my fore-head against it, but only managed to push it away. The end swung round, the fresh chewed wood in my face and I seized the trunk again, this time as if it were a pole. Or a battering ram, which I now found myself pushing forward towards the beavers' quote unquote lodge. I closed my eyes and heaved.

When I opened them, nothing had changed—it was still a heap of shit. Maybe there were a few floating twigs, a dislodged clump of mud and grass slowly sinking to the bottom. Still, the damage had been done.

Decades ago, I had a lover who owned a coat trimmed with beaver skin. The kind inherited from a grandmother, or maybe a grandfather (google "Oscar Wilde in Beaver Fur Coat While Visiting America"). Back in the late seventies, as outerwear tricked out with obviously fake fur trim filled the streets, that coat with its sumptuous strips of authentic pelt drew PETA ire. To the accusations of slaughter, my long ago lover responded: *le dommage a déjà été fait*. An aside: it's funny, how I remember the coat, as well as the unapologetic retort, but not the coat's owner. I'm not even sure whether it was a woman or a man, though the nationality could've been French.

So, the damage had been done. Had already been done: *a déjà été fait*. And not really, as it turned out, by me, much as I would like to erase the tree trunk episode. The next morning, just before the arrival of the mail boat, Kristal knocked on my door and asked to come in. She was wearing the flannel shirt from the day before but her head was uncovered, her hair standing up at the crown in a little boy cowlick. Slung over her shoulder was a knapsack. Setting it on the floor, she sat down in the same chair where my sister had sat two months before and offered to help me get back on my feet. Then she thanked me: you opened my eyes. I noted how once again, body parts provided figurative assistance, while I lay literally in bed.

Not that I wouldn't have opened them myself, eventually. But I was like in some kind of weird fog. You were right about my thesis manuscript. It was never going to happen, even after she finally took it out to her studio. Every time she went to the outhouse, I'd go check to see if she'd started on it. First it was on the far edge of her desk. As if she was quarantining it. Then it was on top of the bookcase. Then it was on the filing cabinet. And then it was gone. The night before last, I finally asked her if she ever planned to read my thesis. You know what she said? That I had my whole academic career ahead of me—years and years to read and write books. But not to make babies, and I'd be such a great mother. We'd both be great parents and she'd pay for everything, beginning with the IVF. I could not believe it at first. Her words were just floating in my head and I couldn't think about what she was saying. Hell it took the rest of the night and most of the next day and that stupid ass hike for the truth to sink in: Irene is just another homesteader, out for the *corn*.

She stood up, hoisting the knapsack, hopefully with her thesis zipped inside (I thought of offering to read it, but my attention span is zero these days), over her shoulder: Well, I can't miss that mail boat. I've got a friend waiting for me over in town.

But before she left, she crossed the room, and setting the knapsack down, bent over my bed and gave me a hug. I held her tight for a moment, the fishing lures with their empty hooks dangling overhead. Then I let my hand play over the knobs of her spine, stray up to that little tuft of hair at the back of her crown. Her weight crushed me down into the bed and she smelled unwashed, like a human body. Like a human body that had done and would continue to do all the things human bodies do—eat, piss, shit, fuck, think. Because the head is part of the body, too. And for the second time, my own mind went blank. My mind went blank even as I felt her lips brush my cheek, heard her whisper in my ear: Crones rule. And then she pulled away.

Crones rule. Do you agree, Madmaeve? *Old's cool*, you wrote in your blog, but maybe the suggestion of sovereignty is a bit much? And if they do rule, then over what? What is their domain? I have no sway anymore, over anyone or anything, least of all, myself. Muscles and ligaments atrophying, bones attenuating, skin slackening, aplomb slipping, restraint cracking—self-governance grows shakier by the day. If you could just see me here in my efficiency unit at the Lincoln Log Motel, heaped all alone on the bed (I lied about Beryl or Darryl, a pornographic attempt to sound less pathetic): it is assisted living, at best. You would never guess at the autonomy that was once mine. That I could, for instance, make myself come, or not, on a dime. Make myself, or for that matter, anyone else—as if I commanded some kind of secret joystick or jubilee button that could, with a simple flick of the wrist or press of the finger, electrify the entire soma.

Twenty odd years ago, Beryl or Darryl, or Beryl *and* Darryl, might've been here with me, though I don't think those were their names. Nor can I recall the title of the conference though I think it had something to do with "queering," back in the days when the word was making its debut as a gerund. I do recall the location—Ithaca,

New York. In fact, the conference per se was at Kristal's alma mater. I also remember the name of the motel on the outskirts of town that the three of us went to afterwards, though never mind about that (the collection agency dogged me for years). I

Editor's Note:
Consider also "quare" or "kwer," a different pronunciation that extends the meaning of "queer" to include the sense of "very/considerable." As in "I'd travel a quare distance to be with ye."

probably shouldn't have allowed the room to go on my credit card—but I was the only one with a tenure-track job, and the desk clerk said he couldn't accept the others' Discover cards. And otherwise, he was conveniently lax—an organic chemistry graduate student, I believe. Studying a big book on isomers, or maybe it was isotopes, in between checkins and checkouts.

Each room had a theme—Venice, Key West, the moon—conveyed through mural wallpaper printed with scenic motifs (gondoliers, palm trees, moon craters). Exotic, far flung locales for just $39.00 per night. Ours, believe it or not, was a woodland paradise —sunlight slanting through pines, mossy stones, etc. In the center there was a king-sized waterbed, covered with a blue sateen spread. I can still feel it on my skin. Already slightly tacky to the touch, by the end of the week the polyester fabric was both gooey and crusty stiff, a supersaturated patchwork of diverse and pluralized ejaculates. Still, if it had been the bedspread and ruined towels alone, I might have gotten away with just the room charges. Or even the graffiti (there was an artist among us, who sharpie penned those forest glades with floating genitalia, for there is no castration).

It was on our final day, an hour or two before check-out, that the waterbed broke. Maybe there was something provoking about that wallpaper with its Disneyfied forest scene, as if there were cartoon critters peering through the trees. Could we make those long lashed eyeballs bulge? Could we make them pop as we rolled onto the floor, slammed up against the walls, careened back onto the roiling rubber surface of the bed (now stripped bare of both sheets and blue sateen), furiously licking, sucking, rubbing, fingering, fisting, though I don't think ever actually fucking, at least in the old school sense, even as I'm pretty sure one of us had a penis? Or maybe we were just performing for each other, an antic play of moist cavities and thrusting appendages without regard for any audience or outside obligations at all. I think someone had a baby somewhere—I heard it crying through the pay-phone outside one evening, on my way to the vending machines—and maybe there was a boyfriend or a girlfriend, a husband or a wife. Yes, maybe we were performing the idea that we could just be bodies, without loyalties or attachments, roles or expectations, histories or futures.

The contents of my suitcase, open on the floor, were soaked. Including a couple of books I'd bought for Kew in an Ithaca bookstore—canine tales, in lieu of the pet she'd

The Bravest Dog Ever: The True Story of Balto, the famously loyal Siberian husky who served his master through thick and through thin, and traveled a quare distance for him. Surely it would be a nice present to receive from your mother.

been pleading for since preschool. I don't remember the titles, though one, I think, began with a "B" and concerned the exploits of a brave and trusty sled dog that saved a town from diptheria. When I got back to Irene and Todd's cabin, late that night, I placed them on top of the wood-stove to dry.

In the morning, while Irene was out splitting wood, I presented the books to Kew. The covers were mottled, the pages warped and swollen. I explained that after the conference I'd gone camping with some colleagues and our kayak had overturned.

She hugged the books to her chest. Her arms were crusted with impetigo scabs and her hair was a mess— clumped and fuzzy. Clearly no one had bothered with the jar of conditioner, not to mention the pick, while I was gone. She fixed me with her big dark eyes, lashes preposterously long: Well I'm glad you're okay, Mommy.

That was my domain, and I trashed it, long ago.

After Kristal left, Irene stayed in her writing studio for the entire day, into the night. By later afternoon, I was starving, so I went up to the main cabin and gathered up some food from the larder: a box of muesli, a wedge of cheddar, a few late season peaches, a carton of almond milk, a small jug of maple syrup. I brought it all back and made myself a meal, which I ate at the little table by the picture window, overlooking the lake. I wondered if I could stay. Already, the days were (are) growing shorter, and I imagined the two of us there, as the summer turned into fall, and fall into winter, each in her separate cabin, Irene with her books and manuscripts, me with the beetles, which though no longer flying about, were surely still there, burrowed in their bark refuge, quietly gestating another outbreak. I left my dinner on the table, and went down to the dock, to smoke a cigarette in the warmth of the setting sun.

When I returned, the steps were covered with syrup and muesli. The screen door, which I'd apparently left unlatched, was wide open. Inside, one raccoon remained. It was sitting on the table, a peach in its paws. Its bright and naturally small eyes were blinking, but not at me. They were focused on the hunk of cheddar, abandoned on the bed.

So now here I am, at the Lincoln Log Motel. I've decided, over these days of ramblings (and thank you for accompanying me, Madmaeve), that I won't be returning to Lake Serene. Rather, I will be moving on to Richfield Springs, NY. Wherever that is. It seems that my former Syracuse brother is now my Richfield Springs brother, due to *good times* he's invited me to share. Better than bad, I suppose, which is all Johnny had to offer the last time around.

Circa 1984, Johnny was in between girlfriends and so were his two housemates, a Syracuse University dropout turned disco dee jay and coke dealer and an ex con who called himself a graduate of Pen State and ostensibly made a living as an auto mechanic specializing in foreign cars. Erick and Derrick might've been their names. Or not. Regardless, they were both dicks. And even that was not necessarily a problem in itself—it was more the fists. More the fists, because though at the time I wasn't one to pull punches (for hadn't Kevin and I lived in battered accord, at least before Belfast?), I've never enjoyed being manhandled. I left the day the ex con told me I'd be a better fuck with fewer teeth, along with less lip.

Johnny's invitation this time came via the internet (only $9.95 extra a day, but it adds up), early this morning. The next bus to Richfield Springs (or rather the general vicinity; there seems to be no direct service) doesn't leave until tomorrow. So in the meantime I'll be packing (leaving these chicos behind for someone more deserving than I to find: may their carefree fabrics and forgiving shapes bring comfort and succor), and checking my email while I've still got service (hint hint).

On Weds, Aug 14th, 2013 at 12:10am, Madmaeve <madmaeve17@gmail> wrote:
Have ye no other kin ye can turn to?

What a question, coming from you, Madmaeve. Didn't you write in your blog, just a month or so ago, before you left home, about *the familial prison#*? About how your sister, having left the *arsehole husband* and returned home to Mammy and Daddy, had no clue? About how she failed to recognize that *family t'is the Long Kesh of heteronormative conformity*? She needs to escape, you wrote, *the barbed wire embrace of kindred who can't afford to be kind.* Indeed, your mammy, rather than loaning your sister money for tuition for a primary school teacher training program, had signed her up instead for free marriage counseling at St. Mary's church, which is nothing, you wrote, *but the socio-theological combination lock for female self-incarceration.* Duh. Finally it was just a matter, you sagely concluded, of *being moved from one cellblock to another.* Or as your mammy apparently put it, *he's your family now.*

I'm guessing that, skimming through my messages (I don't flatter myself that you've actually read them) you caught the glint of a ring. Though Kevin and I never exchanged them and our marriage vows, spoken following a pre-nup weekend of upstate apple picking (me climbing and throwing the apples down to my one-legged beau), in front of a justice of the peace in Poughkeepsie, NY, just a week before our transatlantic flight out of JFK, were not traded in church. Still, the sheet of official foolscap was fetter enough for the folks back in Belfast. Especially with the added link of my new belly—still barely perceptible but in the eyes of Kevin's family and friends, t'was a bond til death did us part. Which is another reason I didn't stick around.

But oh they welcomed me with open (not yet cocked and loaded) arms those Killeens did, the bleary eyed Da (the ma having died some years back after still birthing the last Killeen. *A bad delivery*, the Da told me, as if it had been an ill timed joke), the remaining kids (whose ages ranged from thirty five to ten), the spry maternal Gran Da (technically not a Killeen, but I don't recall a surname), and all the Killeen friends—welcomed me with open arms, heaps of sweets, and jelly jars of Killeen poteen. The celebration lasted all night, *like a good Irish Wake*, one of Kev's old mates declared, *seein' as how we've lost our old friend to this fine feek of a girl*. And after, the craic continued, with daily visits from Kev's sisters, bearing sleeves of biscuits and trays of iced cakes, brewing pot after pot of tea as they giggled in Gaelic over my belly, and thrice weekly evening paramilitary parties, welcoming old friends back home from gaol or sending them off (*say hello to Brendan for us; give Gerry our regards*).

We lived off savings, mostly Kevin's—the pile he'd amassed trading his brogue for tips at Paddy's Midtown Manhattan Pub. The idea was that we'd each, with the low cost of living in a war zone, work on our "art." And at first, Kevin would swing away on his crutches each morning for the Linen Library, to squeeze out a poem or two, before going to meet his pals for an afternoon pint. But soon enough he grew tired of the linguistic struggle, the bloodless scrabble for words. All the other lads were *still out there risking their lives* robbing banks, plundering post offices, pirating trains, planting bombs and picking off Brits, or as he put it, proprietorially patting my abdomen, *making a better world for our weean.* By the time I met Andy, he hadn't written a poem in months.

Largely (and growing ever larger), I spent my days alone, in our three-room garret atop a seedy old villa near the University (away from the bombs if not the bombast, as the students in the flat below us loudly debated politics, both local and global—apartheid was a big topic—day and night). Initially, like Kevin, I dabbled, drawing cavorting human and animal figures in the emerging street-art style that had begun, in the months preceding our departure from New York, to appear on exposed brick, concrete, fiberglass and corrugated steel, and would soon be associated with names like Haring and Basquiat—using the seemingly crude as a short cut to cool until one evening, home early and in a beery piss, Kevin said, flipping through my sketch book, *there's a difference woman, between raw and half baked.* Since the gaggle of Killeen sisters typically didn't arrive until teatime, I had taken to visiting them, lumbering down in the mornings along the

Malone Road, plodding through the Botanic Gardens to a neighborhood of nondescript brick and stucco terrace houses that nevertheless marked the tribal territory of the Killeens.

That had been my intention, the morning Andy appeared, but the rain was not just coming down but sideways, lashing my bare ankles (there were no maternity pants to be found in that city, and I'd never been able to tolerate garter belts, despite their sadomasochistic utility), and finally I'd stumbled back to the flat. Having peeled away my wet clothes and hung them in the bedroom to dry, I'd wrapped myself in my beige rayon maternity kimono (a precursor of the chicos and gift from the Killeen sisters, who claimed it made me look like *a radiant earth mother*) and was now sitting at the kitchen table, splattering black tea on a six-month old copy of the *Village Voice*. Pushing damp strings of hair out my eyes, the underside of my belly brushing the tops of my thighs, I leaned forward, squinting at the photos and pondering. Was that me in my SAMO t-shirt at the Mudd Club? Maybe, maybe not—the image was too grainy to tell. If I wrote my Park Slope brother (the only one in my family with any spare cash) and asked him to send a money order for $500 so that I could buy a plane ticket home, would he? Alas, my recollection of his face the night he came downstairs and discovered me having an after hours soiree in his garden apartment, far sharper than my recall of whomever I was having it with (was it Joan, or Jane, or John? Or perhaps all three?), was all too clear. When suddenly there came a heavy knock at the door, a kind of doggish sliding thump. I hoisted myself up, one hand on the back of the chair, the other pulling my kimono over my abdomen.

Again I squinted, this time through the security peep-hole, expecting to see the top of the landlady's thinning coiffure, pink scalp speckled with dye: the rent was overdue. Instead I saw square commando-sweatered shoulders, which gave rise to a long white neck, laryngeal prominence five or six years past its choirboy peak, I guessed. Wet dark strands of hair obscured the downcast face: brooding or hangdog, I couldn't tell, but either way, there was a certain stray appeal. I slid the bolt and opened the door.

Pushing his wet hair behind his ear, he raised his eyes and almost met mine, his focus gliding up over my face—but then it kept on going, arrested only by the ceiling. It was the sexiest once over I'd ever gotten, a kind of roll that bypassed all earthly foreplay and went straight for ecstasy. I slid my own gaze down the length of him, taking in the way his soaked clothing, the commando style wool pullover and black jeans, molded the lean mongrel lines of him, casting the slight swell of his crotch (briefly, I wondered what his backside looked like), delineating the long bones of his thighs. Water slicked the linoleum surrounding his steel-toed boots.

Is Kevin in? he rasped over my head.

Who was asking?

Andy.

I told him that Kevin wasn't home but that he could come in for some tea if he liked. He hesitated. So I said but you can't go out again all wet like that, and besides I'm expecting Kevin any minute though at that point I would've bet a one-way ticket back to NYC, or at least the free-rider taxing my uterus, that he wouldn't be home until the

94

pubs closed. I stepped to the side motioning the guy in. Affecting to be the little wifey I was not, as he crossed the threshold I told him to take off the boots, and even to drape his socks over the kitchen radiator.

Which smelled like wet animals as they steamed in the heat, like outside things with bits of twig and crumbles of dirt and dung in their fur, brought in. Andy mumbled an apology for the *manky* odor. That was one of Kevin's words, the one he used to describe me when I was menstruating, though that was an inside thing, seeping out. My manky smell had once turned Kevin on, by the way, which was one of the things I'd liked about him, back in New York. His enthusiasm for crossing erotic borders and boundaries. That was all gone in Belfast, where an invisible wall as insurmountable as a peace line barricade separated my half of our shitty little four poster bed (a Killeen family "heirloom") from his. I had assumed the personal was a reflection of the political, now that Kevin was back in his sectarian element, where everything was parceled out into distinct apartheid pieces, and the fucking seemed to be largely linguistic, as in "fucking prods." Now, looking at mongrel Andy, slumped sideways in a chair, his gaze no longer directed toward the ceiling, but down at his own bare feet, I wondered. He was clearly uncomfortable with me—yet the smell of sex was on him, as pungent as his socks. I bustled around, filling the electric kettle with water for tea, putting out a plate of McVities, using my bulk as a kind of reassurance, as an evocation of everywoman (mother, sister, daughter, wife), an abstraction of feminine succor sanitized of all personal stink. Despite a capacity for raunch that was surely greater than his own and Kevin's combined.

I poured the hot water into the brown glazed crockery teapot, another Killeen family cast-off, then set it on the table with a second mug for Andy. He was still staring down at his feet, which were bone thin and motionless on the floorboards, like long, taxidermied paws. I lowered myself back into my chair, the seat creaking as I sat. Biting into a McVities, I lingered for a few more moments on the photo of the Mud Club (according to in the column beneath, *all the village people* were there that night), then folded up the paper and pushed it away. When I looked again at Andy, I saw that his lips were moving though the only sound in the room was the tick tick of the cheap windup clock on the shelf over the cast iron sink. Noiselessly muttering he lifted his hands in front of his face, wiggling his long fingers and waving his palms in what appeared to be some sort of evocation or strange prayer, even as his gaze remained on his feet. And then suddenly the ticking of the clock on the shelf behind me was subsumed by a thumping, vibrating the floor beneath table. I craned in my seat and saw the balls of Andy's feet doing a rapid slap slap against the floor, a flesh pedal pumping as if he was priming himself to bolt.

In any downtown bar or club, back in Alphabet City, I would've spelled it out immediately. But in Belfast, the late seventies seemed coincident with the late fifties in America, "Happy Days" reborn in the midst of the Troubles, complete with black leather jackets, cock hugging jeans and beer with whiskey chasers. Minds here had not been altered, as far as I could tell, since the Plantation of Ulster—and alcohol was the common lubricant that preserved the narrow channels of both Taig and Prod.

Since my arrival, I'd had nothing else (Kevin's sisters proclaiming the benefits of stout in particular for the unborn bairn), and tired as I was of booze, it had begun to taste like the only choice. I'd forgotten that there were other drugs to do.

Abruptly the thumping of Andy's feet ceased, as suddenly as it had begun. He raised his head and his hands floated away from his face, fingers still wiggling, drifting towards the brown crockery teapot. With hovering hands, he stared down at it, pupils dilated, lips parted in apparent wonder. Then he recited, *why here is the girl's head, like an exhumed gourd...*

Before I discuss the poetry, a few words about the pottery. The teapot, according to one of the Killeen sisters, had been presented by a visiting American relative as a hostess gift to their late mother: a round cheeked smiling visage was stamped into its earthenware curvature. The face was identical to the faces on the pottery sun ornaments that presided over seventies patios in the United States (my Brooklyn brother and sister-in-law had one affixed to the garden wall behind their brownstone), perhaps manufactured in the same Mexican ceramics factory, only it had been glazed a subterranean brown rather than solar yellow, as if to cater to the non-heliophiles in the export market.

As for the poetry, you'll perhaps recognize it, Madmaeve, as being from Northern Ireland's poet laureate, specifically as a line from one of the "Bog Poems," which had in part inspired Kevin's return (though Belfast born and bred, the only quagmire he'd ever set his foot in was political). Later, Andy would tell me that it was

Seamus Heaney who had brought them together: Kevin having tripped over him in the stacks of the Linen Library, sprawled asleep on the floor with a volume of *North* spread face down over his chest. And I would also learn that Andy was not in fact the mongrel or stray that I'd initially perceived him as, but merely a runaway, most recently returned from rooming with a cousin in London, who when they'd lost the squat to a developer, had sent him back to Belfast with a care package of hallucinogens. Andy definitely had a home—a home where the "dirty taig poet's" works were forbidden by his English ancestry touting mum (who'd nailed a small tin coat of arms to the battered security door of their Shankill Road walkup), and Wordsworth and Tennyson spouting dad (who'd long ago purchased the collected Everyman's Library works of each with the intention of pursuing a degree in English literature at Queens, only too many filthy fenians had already infiltrated the program).

There was no provision of background or exposition that morning, however, though the bog motif persisted. Andy touched the teapot, traced the curve of its smile with a black rimmed fingernail: *Did the fen eat ye darlin,' all but yer sweet head?* His finger dialed up and around, lightly circling the ceramic cheek, then swooped down the bridge of the ceramic nose, resting there tip to tip. I felt my nipples harden and my clitoris begin to throb.

No, I said, taking hold of his hand. I'm still here. And I put his hand on my breast, which with pregnancy had become an erogenous zone like never before. I slid his palm over the round swollen bub with its nipple spout, like a carnal teapot, and cupped it beneath, making him hold the fleshy weight. Then I guided it out of the groove between breast and abdomen, pulling it down and up over the curve of my belly, which had become an erogenous zone as well. Actually, my entire body had become one, every surface, every fold, every cavity. I pressed his hand to my belly, and he made no effort to remove it though he had yet to look at me. I could smell his lanolin steeped sweat seeping through the underarm of his pullover, but otherwise he was stone still—all the fidgeting, fluttering and thumping had ceased. When finally he whispered, Och, tis the Bog Queen herself.

Whether he actually perceived me as such or was simply playing along, he never said. I'm guessing the veil of hallucinogens did their part, along with the cerement beige of the kimono and the swollen mass it covered—no doubt I looked like I'd been buried for five hundred years in a swamp, mud-leached, waterlogged and pulp-soft. But Bog Queen or bloated mammy-to-be, my power over him was now absolute. I hoisted myself up, told him to re-bolt the door (just in case the Killeen sisters came knocking, though they'd never arrived before four), and then pulled him to the back room and the fourposter bed, his head down like a dog on a leash, though he padded after me willingly enough.

I made him undress, and then I asked him to turn around so that I could see the backside of him. I was not disappointed. Unlike the majority of Belfast boyos I'd seen, including the males in the Killeen tribe, with the exception of Kevin himself, Andy actually had an ass, each cheek bringing yet another absorbing convexity to the table, or in this case, the bed. I didn't look for long, however, at least not that day. I was so wet that I could feel the seepage runneling down over my perineum and soaking the coverlet beneath my thighs. So wet that as I glanced past Andy to the window behind him, the wash of rain over the panes seemed like a correlative of my flow.

At almost eight months, counting the days, the positions open to me were few. In fact, given my great and tender girth, there was only one, so that now I was the dog, forearms and shins firmly planted into the mattress, my rump in the air. Even now, decades later, I can remember that first thrust, that searing leap that sent seismic waves roiling in my groin, though such was the kid's finesse (perfected, he later told me, during his stretch in London town), that I didn't actually come until he began pumping his muck inside me, panting, I'm sinkin', I'm sinkin', I'm sinkin'... I'm sunk.

Afterwards, he was still high, or low, as he lay on his back, his hands folded over his only half flaccid cock, his eyes blank as pools as he muttered about the *tawny rut* and the *wettish shaft*, about *souterrain flow*. So I helped him dress and sent him off—in my advanced state of pregnancy I really didn't have the stamina for another round, anyway. And I didn't expect to see him again, after what I assumed had been a onetime drug directed diversion. Not only was I grotesquely gravid, but I was not, I suspected, the sex he usually sought. I assumed he'd been hooking up with Kevin in the jakes at the back of the pub, and would resume that activity. I didn't realize that first day, having no eye for or interest in political niceties, that Andy came from a Unionist background, and was thus mortally unwelcome in Republican establishments, off license or not. Indeed, Andy would later inform me, there'd been nothing going on, for lack of a suitable venue for getting it on. T'was his acid addled brain and Kevin piqued cock that had led him to our door the first time, he said, but it was *the slime kingdom* of my cunt that brought him back.

The very next morning, in fact. And the morning after that. On the third day, Andy broke one of the headboard posts of the shitty four poster, grabbing it for support as he shifted my hips for a better angle of entry, and on the sixth day, together we collapsed the bed entirely, yet every day for the next ten days he returned, including Sunday, after Kevin's departure for mass, ever more brazen in his craze for my snatch. And every day that doggish sliding thump on the door triggered a gush between my legs so that on the tenth day, when my water broke, I assumed that it was the usual welcoming flow. Only when it became clear that my contractions were prohibiting further ingress, and that someone else had to come out before Andy could get in again, did I finally tell him to go. Since I had no phone in the flat, I asked him to stop by the cabstand on the Lisburn Road on his way home and send over a car.

Strangely, none of the neighbors noticed Andy's comings and goings. Or maybe not so strangely—they were students after all, preoccupied with their own polemics, amorous as well as political (as evidenced by the early morning floor swaps I'd witnessed on my way down to empty the rubbish in the dustbin). Rather, it was one of the drivers at the cabstand, a crony of Kevin's, who recognized the address, and wondered how the young snout had come to know it, too.

The evening after I returned home from the maternity ward, Kevin inquired about my *visitor*. Sprawled in the former four poster turned three, my crotch sore with the needlework of the obstetrician, the baby to my side querulous with hunger in its bassinet beribboned by the Killeen sisters—I was a sampler portrait of feminine abjection, stitched in the stagnant hours of postpartum depression. I looked up at him, hanging on his crutches by my bedside, yet in no way hindered in his comings and goings, swinging out the door and back in again, whenever he goddamn pleased. It would've been so easy to say that *Andy came looking for you,* since after all he had, at least the first time, two weeks ago. Perhaps there'd even been an assignation planned, for the hours of my daily morning visit with Kevin's sisters. And why not? Hadn't we both once been Catholic in our tastes and sexual practices, and now that I was necessarily barred from broader pursuits by maternal convention, why shouldn't Kevin carry on? It would've been so simple to add, with a knowing wink, *I think he was hoping to find you home alone.* But I did not. Instead, I said, yeah, the kid was coming over every day, fucking my brains out.

Back in New York, Kevin would have jumped my bones, right then and there, lunging, digging, dredging and wresting, as if to rout the scent of Andy while it was still warm. But in Belfast, he simply stood frozen by my bedside, face reddening, nostrils twitching. Of course, the baby might have had something to do with it, too—maybe my maternity had made me tainted quarry, too taboo to touch. Regardless, as he slowly crossed his arms over his chest, jaw tight and lips pursed, it was clear that he was no longer my kinky, stink chasing Kev-boy, but an upstanding Daddy-man, preparing to issue his dictum. I stared back at him, raising an eyebrow: what would it be, "bitch," "cunt" or "whore" (or "whoor-uh," as he used to say)?

It was number three, though it sounded more like "haur" this time, as if his throat was congested with rage.

You haur, he spat. You filthy feckin' cock hoppin' haur that's what you are. I made you my wife and brought you home to my family only to learn that you're not a woman but an animal—you've no sense of human decency a'tall. And then he left, slamming the security door behind him. As he trundled down the stairs, the baby began to wail.

That was the last I saw of Kevin: one of the Killeen sisters identified the body, which was too battered by the beating to permit an open casket at the wake. Cloaked in my widowhood, Kevin's kid clutched like a Kevlar shield to my breast, I did gather bits and pieces as I wandered the room, which allowed me to visualize his final movements, including his efforts to cover his own erotic tracks: *T'was at the pub that night that he told us...apparently she met the prod pouf at the Linen Library...Gay as the day is long, I heard...An innocent enough beginning though you have to wonder about her hoofin' all the way down there in her condition...Just poetry it twas ...But ye don't go readin' poetry to another man's wife, especially in his own home...Kev only meant to give the wee prick a warnin'... Fair enough...If only*

*he'd brought along a few mates, instead of ragin' over to
Shankill to confront the scut all on his own...They say our
man never even caught up with the orangey fairy—t'was the
street brigade that got him...Away in the head our Kev must've
been for her...An insult to be sure, but t'was only poetry...She
ain't worth it, if you ask me...True. But surely she was a glorious ride, before Kev knocked her up.*

I marveled at Kevin's presence of mind in first dissem-
inating a story so clearly in service of his cock; I was certain that the reason he'd gone seeking our randy Andy
on his own was to give the boy's ass a good private back
alley thrashing. And thanks to Kevin's more or less per-
suasive performance of the aggrieved paterfamilias, I was
more or less safe. All I had to do was to keep a low profile, crouching beneath my widow's crape. Hide the ride
that had never stopped revving, glorious or not. And in
the meantime I would plan my getaway. This time when I
wrote my Brooklyn brother, I sent a clipping from the *Belfast Telegraph* about "the deadly sectarian beating," along
with a few words about my concern for my own safety
and the baby's (though already I was planning on leaving
it behind, as a parting gift to the Killeens), since Kevin's
murderers were still at large.

As I waited for my brother's response, the days grew
longer and the rain became less constant, the sky clearing
for hours at a time, blessing Belfast with its blotless blue.
One morning I awoke in the three poster, to sun streaming through the window and the Killeen baby, which just
hours earlier had been screeching and scrabbling at my
breast, as I tried to plug the bottle in its mouth, lying
on its back beside me, still as an egg but for the gentle

lifting of its chest. I felt something stir inside me, a hankering for something beyond the walls of the flat where I'd been holed up for months. The phrase *kick up your heels* popped into my head though I'd probably never used it in my life, and soon I found myself bouncing the big rubber wheeled perambulator (another Killeen hand-me-down) down the Malone road. I'd even brought my sketchbook along, having tucked it into the nylon pocket behind the pram's hood.

In the Botanic Park, I spotted an unoccupied bench in front of a row of hedges flowered with clusters of tiny white blossoms. Bits of bread littered the gravel in front of the bench, the remains of someone's breakfast bun. As I parked the pram on the gravel in front of the bench I caught a strong, fetid odor—— and I realized that the smell was wafting over from the flowered hedges. I considered moving on to find another bench, but the Killeen baby, which had begun to stir as I'd entered the park, whimpering if not yet squalling, had suddenly gone quiet, its squirming form, inert. So I sat down, closed my eyes and tilted my face to the morning sun. The smell of the hedges was unsettling, simultaneously arousing and repellent. It was like sex and the

Tis the *manky* scent of the whitethorn or in proper Irish, *skeogh*—variously known by yousuns as hawthorn, thorn, thornapple, may-tree, quickthorn, mayblossom, hawberry, hedgethorn, bread and cheese tree, lady's meat and hagthorn—is a confusin' one to mortal sniffers. As is what to make of the plant itself! Some believe that sittin' beneath a whitethorn tree means ye will meet a certain folk, while others believe it provides protection from same: *Creep under the thorn/it will save you from harm.* Tis a gateway tree (or hedge) to be sure, which is not to be confused with a gateway drug!

end of sex, like a cunt full of jism and a spade full of dirt, and I wondered what the hedges were as well as what sort of flying thing the flowers attracted, if any. This was no smell for the birds and the bees. Would Kevin have known? Probably not. The botanical world had held no more interest for him than a convenience store, its products provoking incurious appreciation, at most. Sampling cider in a gift shop during our upstate apple picking expedition, he'd been surprised to learn that it came from apples—not a tap at a bar. *Christ*, he'd complained, *ye can't even pull a buzz out of that plant piss.* I missed Kevin, or at least the Kevin for whom nothing had existed but as a potential means to get off.

I inhaled, taking in the smell of the white flowered hedges that was like sex and like the end of sex, like the smell that had wafted up from Kevin's grave at the Belfast City Cemetery. I missed Kevin and regretted his death but that didn't mean that I would never have sex with anyone, ever again. In fact I could probably have it with Andy another time or two, if wanted, before I left. Just a few nights ago I'd seen him through the window, standing in the yellow glow of the streetlamp, staring fixedly up at the flat. Staring as if readying to propel himself up and through the panes in a shower of shattering glass. But for me, the frenzy, the frantic urge, the short-circuiting of all foresight and inhibition—that was gone. At least for now. I'd pulled the shade and gone to bed, saving myself for less risky lovers (safe sex practitioners or no), back home.

And then I heard a small choked breathing, a narrow snorting and chuffing noise, a little mouth gasping and panting. I opened my eyes and peered into the pram, but the Killeen baby was still peacefully sleeping, its features shadowed by the hood. And anyway, the noise was coming from the other side of the bench, though now it was more of a scrambling and scuffling, the source of which exploded into view, a twisting, shifting flurry of russet pelted limbs and torsos, long black tipped ears and bobbed white tails, which a second or two later resolved into two rabbits, the largest and leanest I'd ever seen, bigger than the Killeen baby, and way more active, as they reared up and began jabbing at each other with stiff prong-like forearms, mouths closed, faces expressionless, like furry gimp masks with holes cut for the unblinking golden eyes.

The fight or whatever it didn't last long: a magpie swooped down, after a bit of nearby bread, and both rabbits bolted, in opposite directions. One disappeared entirely into a clump of pink flowering shrubs that looked like rhododendrons, further along the path, while the other remained in sight. It stood on its hind legs and sniffed, and after a moment or two loped in the direction of the rhododendrons or whatever they were, vanishing after its fellow into the foliage. I turned and pulled my sketchbook out of the pocket of the pram, intending to sketch the boxing rabbits from memory.

When I looked up again, I saw that they were back. And now both were stationed about fifteen feet away from where I sat, in a circle of mown grass on the other side of the path, one atop the other, still but for the upper's hips, juddering like an engine. For less than thirty seconds they stayed like that, and then they broke apart, each halting a few yards away from the spot of their tryst, nibbling at the grass as if nothing had transpired between them at all. But a little while later, they were at it again, even as the mounted rabbit continued to pluck at the grass, seemingly oblivious to the frenetic pumping of the other. Like before, the coital connection lasted less than half a minute and both rabbits fell to grazing until, as if responding to some internal cue or timer, the one hopped back to the other and resumed its rapid fire rutting. This continued six times more, and though I didn't have a watch, it seemed to me that I could anticipate the length of the intervals between the matings as well the length of the matings themselves, as if the whole process was entirely mechanical and automatic, a Claymation animal sexscapade, like some obscene battery commercial, played over and over again. Though these rabbits, unlike any I had ever seen back home, were no bunnies.

Hares, I suddenly realized. They were hares. But in the end, just one remained on the green, the other having gone off again into the flowering shrubs which probably weren't rhododendrons because the flowers were too small, just as the Killeen baby woke up and began to cry. A single, solitary hare. I don't know which one it was, the male or the female, the top or the bottom, it could've been either—I couldn't tell. The hare went on nibbling at the grass as the Killeen baby cried, louder and louder, its keen **wracking** the soft spring air.

Ach, we're not bitter, not bitter a'tall. Bout ye?

108

On Mon, Jan 6, 2014 at 12:10am, Madmaeve <mad-maeve17@gmail> wrote:

Well it sounds like yer in a tight spot. I wish ye the best.

A tight spot. Yes, you could call it that—literally. I would guess the floor dimensions to be no more than ten feet by ten feet, though the walls are obscured by these stacks of boxes, making the actual boundaries of the room uncertain. I am more confident in my estimation of the ceiling. About twelve feet, I'd say, more than twice my height, if I could stand straight. If this room were clear of boxes, it would be spacious enough, as large or larger than the bedroom I slept in at Grace's house. It could even, in its loftiness, accommodate a loft bed (though that structure would reduce the light from the skylight, the only source of illumination). As it is, there is only enough floor clearance for a twin size mattress in the center, and for a little pathway from the center to the door (too narrow for my crutches, in fact. I have to push and slide them ahead, hopping along behind, to get out). Fortunately the surrounding boxes are not uniformly stacked floor to ceiling. This provides a roomier feel, and also makeshift shelves, ledges and props for personal items, which though fewer than before are easier to sort through when you can see them.

Leaning against one of the stacks of boxes there is a camera tripod. I use it to hang my underpants to dry, after I wash them in the janitor's closet down the hall. There is also, on the cardboard ledge just above it, a vintage Mamiya camera. I like to think that its old fashioned lens is a spy cam, that somewhere someone is watching me, considering my every move. I like to think, but I don't believe, unlike the old woman I see on the sidewalk outside the deli downstairs, muttering into her motheaten fur collar about *medical surveillance*, that someone actually is. What I do believe is that paranoia is the province of the marginalized: when you know, deep down, that no eyes are upon you, you invent them. But I'm not crazy. Yet.

I know nobody's looking, maybe not even you, Madmaeve, despite (or because of) your meager emails. And yet I continue as if I might be seen. And not just here now, on this mattress, my back supported by the box that serves as a headboard, sore coccyx cushioned by the pillow beneath my buttocks, laptop propped against my good thigh (the other prone and seeping through its bandage), but before now and so beyond now. I continue with this story even though maybe the only eyes looking are my own and the only person that I will convince my life happened is me.

When the Adirondack Trailways bus finally reached the closest stop to Richfield Springs, a touristy lakeside village known for its summer cultural scene about fifteen miles away, I had been on it for fourteen hours and fifty five minutes (that does not include the sixteen hours and twenty five minutes I spent languishing overnight in the bus station in Albany, NY). In Irene's pick-up, the journey surely would've taken no more than four hours. But rural buses do not just go—they also stop, in every godforsaken hamlet and four corners along the way. Our route included twenty-one stops (twenty-one opportunities for passengers to lumber on and off, and lumber on again to check for forgotten valuables) that I'm sure, connecting the dots from an aerial view, would've resembled the web of a spider on drugs. As, by the way, a number of my fellow travellers appeared to be—either twitchily staring out the windows, or out cold, nubbly toothed mouths agape. The notable exception was my seatmate from Schroon Lake to Malta, a bright-eyed brat who claimed to be escaping from *juvie*, and who said that on first sight, he'd mistaken me for his Uncle Gordon. *Scared the shit out of me—I thought he was dead.* The kid's misattribution of identity may have had something to do with my dress. Or rather pants. I was wearing a white t-shirt and a pair of khaki tan overalls I'd lifted from the clothesline the morning I left Irene's. Carhartts, in fact.

All this is to say that by the time I staggered out of the bus into the early evening air of the touristy lakeside village, I was a wreck. I hadn't slept or washed in over thirty hours and the tan carhartts were soiled with sundry vending machine snacks and drinks. And of course I must've reeked of the industrial strength disinfectant that saturates all bus deplorables, no matter where their journeys begin or where they end.

My brother was standing with one foot up on the single bench that marked the stop, and as I stepped down out of the bus onto the grassy curb, he continued to look at the exit behind me, clearly waiting for someone else to emerge. He was wearing an Irish fisherman's sweater (which was something of a sartorial surprise) and with his thick spray of silver hair and lean tanned into-the-wind body he looked like he still had a lover in every port. Though as I recalled, his vehicle of choice had always been a motorcycle, not a boat.

Johnny, I called. I saw his eyes jolt with recognition and then as if to obliterate the sight before him he rushed forward and wrapped me in his wiry arms.

He smelled the opposite of disinfectant—of clean fleece and meadow flowers and what I imagined as salt mist though since the nearest ocean was hundreds of miles off, it was probably just sweat. Clean fresh sweat. I belonged back on that bus, but it was already pulling away, air brakes releasing with a hiss. Something prickled against my collarbone and as I extricated myself from my brother's embrace, a sprig of white fell to the ground. Queen Anne's Lace. In late summer in rural New York, you see it everywhere, rioting along the roadsides and in the fields.

Leaving the sprig of white florets to lie on the sidewalk between us, he took hold of my hand, held it up, though stopped short of twirling me around: Look at you. Just look at you, you look like a kid in those farmer pants.

But he couldn't. He could not, or would not look at me, or even past me—his eyes slid down to the flower, as if some other, less repugnant version of me might rest there. As a boy, he'd swaggered with his little buddies through a repertoire of cocksure roles—cowboy, motocross rider, rock star—mini performances of machismo enacted with toy guns, schwinn bikes and air guitars. *Jack the Lad*, our da used to call him. Or sometimes the *Wee Gombeen-Man*, as he persuaded the other lads to wheedle actual equipment out of their fathers—e.g. a Fender Stratocaster which he then "borrowed" until our da found it hidden under his bed. Now he was Gentleman Jack, suavely playing the gallant to my old (bag) lady, only he couldn't quite carry it off.

You're gonna love Grace, he said, turning away to hoist my duffle over his shoulder. Just be yourself Sis, and everything will be fine.

The woman waiting at the car, parked on a side street around the corner from the bus stop, did not share Johnny's ocular inhibition. I assumed this was Grace, who eyed me steadily as we approached, dragging on a cigarette. So I stared back in turn. Like my brother, she wore a white fisherman sweater, and as we drew closer, I could see white sprigs of queen anne's lace stuck into the weave, like floral doilies embossed on top of the cable knit. A pair of mirrored sunglasses dangled from the neckline. Unlike my brother, she was still young—no older, I guessed, than thirty-five or maybe forty. So this was Johnny's good times, his Richfield richesse. Yet she was, despite the pastoral surfeit of her sweater, the opposite of country. Long unwholesomely thin body leaning back against a dirty white SUV, one hand draped over the driver's side mirror, the other pinching the joint, unsmiling face pallid yet electrified by her jet black shag, she was an urban sylph, a Mapplethorpe epicene.

She dropped the cigarette, ground it out in the gutter with the sole of a leather loafer the same dirty white as the car. Then she slipped on the sunglasses before returning her gaze to me. The lenses were large and mirrored. If I saw a Mapplethorpe, did she see an Arbus? Or had my freakishness exceeded the frame altogether? I felt my belly straining against the bib of my carhartts. The bus was gone but I still had the Trailway's regional schedule that I'd stuffed in the thigh pocket. I was about to pull it out when she leaned in and took my hand, as Johnny had done, though without lifting it into the air. It was larger than mine, long and capable looking, nails painted black, even as, grasping my palm, it shook slightly. Heroin withdrawal, I assumed—it fit like an opioid in its receptor. No doubt that was the reason for the shades as well. She was taller than I and as she leaned in I caught the sparkle of something nestled in her collarbone, a diamond, small but brilliant and strung on a fine choker chain. Marian's ring flashed in my mind, and it occurred to me that this woman could be her younger sister, though when the woman spoke, it was from the other side of the Atlantic:

Finally I get ta meet the amazing sister!

Her accent was hardcore New Jersey, laced with ingratiation. With it, she shifted from Mapplethorpe epicene to mall doll anorexic, from cool smack addict to boxed wine sot. I imagined her wheedling prescription drugs from her doctor or bargaining for lower rates with the cable company. And I wondered if money was the measure of my amazingness. In my email correspondence with Johnny I'd suggested that I had some, or would—a forthcoming settlement from the University (*hush money*, I'd told him, just like they gave the football coaches, to prevent another scrimmage in the media, down the line). What would happen when he (or they) found out that I had nothing beyond social security and the single digit thousands, rapidly dwindling (the count down began with those chicos), that I'd managed to salvage from the sale of my house?

But maybe money wasn't it. The ornament on the hood of Grace's mud spattered SUV indicated some expensive make or another. And as I hefted myself up into the front passenger seat, at Grace's insistence and with Johnny's assistance, the snazzy dashboard LCD screens suggested a newer model of whatever expensive make that was. After strapping me in and closing the heavy door with a discrete thud, Johnny got into the back: No worries, Sis. I made Grace buy this baby with plenty of leg room.

In the driver's seat, Grace pushed the ignition button with a long trembling finger, summoning the engine into quiet, well-engineered service—suddenly more dowager than suburban druggie. Then again, the nail was ragged and flaking black polish. She turned slightly and smiled at me as she shifted the car into drive, inscrutable in her mirrored shades as an offshore bank account.

With Irene there had been, so I assumed, at least the concept of sisterhood, in the political if not the biological sense. But what motivated my brother and his Jersey bred benefactress, if not money? I stared out at the white spattered green fields flowing by the window. If you pull up a queen anne's lace plant, you will find a dirty carrot at the root.

In the car, Johnny and Grace discussed the menu for the weekend (a cooler full of farm stand comestibles sat in the back, it seemed), the company (Art and Russell, friends of my brother, would be joining us), and the problems the current power outage at the house, caused by a recent storm, would pose for entertaining said company if it wasn't resolved soon (The NYSEG CEO was a buddy of Art's and Johnny would be giving him a call if those bozos weren't there tomorrow by 9am sharp). I counted collapsed barns.

I'd seen three when Grace asked me if I'd ever met Andy Warhol, or been to his studio.

I had not, I replied (though a former lover of mine used to see him regularly at mass). I do, however, have a memory of waking up early one morning at the Factory. A memory that is possibly false, since I was tripping that night and it could be that I manufactured the silver tinsel, fractured mirrors and famous red couch inside my own head.

So you're interested in Warhol? I looked over at her, at her big hands (now still) on the steering wheel, her face obscured by the oversized sunglasses, like the merchandise behind a darkened shop window. What could this woman possibly have to do with conceptual art? She nodded, but did not elaborate and in her silence she seemed older and earthier—the close-lipped peasant hoarding her meager store of words. So that once again my perspective of her shifted and I saw those big hands scrabbling for an onion in hard, stony ground. Maybe, as heroin addicted Jersey heiress gave way to a middle-aged Italian widow after the second world war (the shakes attributable to shell shock), Cindy Sherman was the answer. Ha.

With whom, it turned out, Grace was familiar (ha on me). She had simply been formulating her thoughts. Now, a monologue ensued, revealing that not only did she know all about Warhol, whom she worshipped as *Gawd*, because after him *anything and everything could be art*, but she was an acolyte of the Pictures Generation. In fact, she credited the mutating B-movie women portrayed in Sherman's *amazing feminist un-selfies*, which she'd first seen during a trip to the city sponsored by her ex-husband's construction company, for opening her eyes about her marriage: I realized I'd been trained from when I was a little girl by all these pictures, all these images, of how I was supposed to be, and what I was supposed to see...

Good for you, I said, shining her on. I felt like I was back in the classroom again, waving the glow stick of feminist approval. I glanced back at my brother, who was bent over his cell phone, and heard the ding of a text coming in, reception undeterred, it seemed, by hinterland forest and field.

I loved art in high school, Grace continued. I was always drawing and taking pictures with this old Mamiya from my grandpa. I even got a partial tuition scholarship, to study art at Pratt. But where was the rest supposed to come from, ya know? So I waited tables every night and took out loans until my ma got sick and I had to go home to help out. And then she died and when I got back I was way behind on everything, course work, projects, and I'd used up all my loan money for the year helping with the funeral expenses and I had no fucking idea how I was gonna pay tuition the next semester, let alone buy art supplies. So one evening this cute guy walks into the steak house, he's a senior business major at Rutgers home for Thanksgiving vacation and he's got all the right lines including the job at his dad's construction company after graduation while I've got all the debt and we go together like a burger and fries. Yada yada yada, we all know the score, like it's right up there on the TV over the bar.

She turned the SUV off of whatever country road we'd been traveling onto a graveled drive and began to ascend through woodland. Without asking, she opened the windows: Just smell the air up here, Sandra. I tell ya, it's saved my life.

I smelled the usual woodland smells: herbal, fungal, decompositional. But at least she hadn't said anything about balsamifers. How long did it last? I asked.

Twenty three years.

The SUV bounced a bit, going over what felt like a rock or a rut but made the sound of cracking wood. I glanced in the side mirror and saw a litter of leaves and branches in the road behind us.

But I don't regret them, Grace resumed. Even though I was living someone else's life it was still mine, ya know? Like just because you're trapped in some image, some lie, it doesn't mean real things aren't happening. I loved my kids, even Mike for most of it. But then the kids went off to college and Mike, my Gawd, it was like he had the master key to bastardom. If it hadn't been painful, literally, it would've been boring. So I got a good lawyer and afterwards my little sister on Wall Street invested the money in stocks and real estate for me and I got lucky. And now I can buy all the art supplies I want.

You should see her photographs, Sis. Cutting edge, cutting edge, my brother said. I looked back, saw he'd put his phone away and assumed there was no cell reception in this corridor through the trees. She even had a show over in Utica.

Grace smiled over at me: If ya think they're crap, Sandra, say it. I won't be offended.

Outside, the setting sun laser pointed the forest floor, marking the leaf mulch with circlets of red. What if I did think Grace's photographs were crap—did she really want to hear that? Again, I wondered what my brother had said about me, and why I had been invited—useless, overeducated bitch that I was (am). Or as an old lover once put it (in fact, I think it was Kew's father): *You say anything but you do nothing, Sandra Dorn.*

Grace's *place*, as my brother called it, was actually an estate, situated at the top of the hill. *Is* an estate, with a name recorded in the New York State Registry of Historic Homes, even though in a short time it will no longer be Grace's. In fact, it was Johnny who drew my attention to the official name of the estate, leaning forward from the back seat to point at the engraved brass plaque on the lintel over the stone gate: *Sunset Hall.* So called, he explained, for the westward facing aspect of the estate house, by the *Revolutionary War entrepreneur* who had commissioned it. *Sadly*, the man, *passed away* just as the interior *finishing touches* were completed.

Maybe Daddy Warbucks should've had it turned the other way and called it Sunrise Hall instead, Grace commented.

Mowed lawn rolled away from either side of the drive, heaped here and there with storm debris, scattered like bodies on a battlefield. Swallows or bats (we'd reached that transitional hour between the day shift insectivores and the night) darted and swooped overhead and the air streaming in now smelled of cut grass comingled with mineralized decay, a graveyard scent that intensified as we drew up before a giant limestone portico flanked by two stories of black, door-sized windows, most of them boarded over. Grace put the car in park, keeping the engine running. She had taken off her sunglasses, which were once again hooked over the collar of her sweater, but her face remained unreadable as she gazed up at her *place*.

Johnny, still leaning forward, forearms draped over our seats, one hand resting on Grace's shoulder, the other on mine, rattled on: Fifty rooms but only one bathroom. I'm not kidding. All the interior walls are solid fieldstone, built to accommodate all the future Warbucks, but forget about modern plumbing and wiring. Unless you can think outside the box, or actually inside it, like I have. See I've got this idea to build conventional sheet rock and plaster walls within the walls that are already there. People don't want those huge rooms anymore, they want the scale to be more human like. Also you'll have a better insulated and more energy efficient structure over all. A win win. Now I'm looking into getting some guys on board to finance the renovation and turn it into a boutique hotel, with a gallery space for Gracie's photographs. It shouldn't be a hard sell: upstate just keeps getting hipper all the time.

I noted Johnny's use of the first person, even as I guessed that Grace alone had bought the estate. His salaried jobs—roadie, bartender, cook, construction worker, bartender, carpenter, bartender—had never afforded him more than a Triumph motorcycle and a Bambi travel trailer. And while he'd maintained a sideline over the years as a ladykiller, not one of his victims, as far as I knew, had put him in her will. But Grace seemed unbothered by and even oblivious to his pronominal presumption: whatever, Johnny Boy. Just keep 'em out of the carriage house, okay?

The carriage house. Set against a backdrop of woods, two hundred yards or so behind the estate house, it was a barn shaped building with a covered flagstone terrace extending from the westward side. In the almost dark, unlit by exterior porch bulb or interior lamp, it crouched beneath the canopy of pines like some big haunched animal, ready to pounce or maybe bolt. I trailed Grace and Johnny over the needle carpeted ground up onto the flagstone and watched Grace fumble with her key at the screen door.

Inside, she picked up a flashlight from a little entryway table and flicked it on. Her face was pale as putty, her eyes dark and glittering in the back glow: Ta da.

She swept the LED beam from one end of the interior to the other, delineating a large open area huddled here and there with assorted chairs, sofas and coffee tables, like a hotel lobby or salon, then swung it up first laterally to spotlight the barn doors on one side of the room, above which a big paned window displayed the crescent moon, to a fireplace on the other with a gun hung just a foot or so above the mantel and a zebra pelt affixed to the wall just over it (the decor here seemed to be causally connected), then longitudinally to show what appeared to be loft spaces at either end, though there were no visible stairs or ladders to access them: I think this main room must be where they kept the carriages and wagons. Like a big garage, ya know? But then they needed places for the horses and gear.

She shifted the beam to the plastered wall to the left of the fireplace, revealing a closed door, then to the right, showing another door, and another beyond that, and then two more around the corner: Four of those are bedrooms and that one there is the kitchen, but I'm pretty sure that originally there were stalls and tack rooms all around. Cool, huh?

I heard Johnny make a little noise behind me, a sigh or a snort.

And up there, she continued, directing the beam to one of the loft spaces above, is where they kept the hay. Because there were still some old bales up there when we had insulation and an attic fan put in, so that I can use it as a darkroom. But that's all we're gonna do, right Johnny? I wanna keep this wonderful house just like it is, when they made it into a summer cottage, back in the nineteen fifties.

Johnny brushed past me, encircled Grace with one arm and kissed the top of her head. The flashlight dangled from her hand, spotlighting her feet, slim and girlish in the dirty white loafers, next to his, broad and dad-like in new looking khaki cross-trainers. What had my brother worn in the footloose days of yore? Scuffed motorcycle boots came to mind.

You sure, Gracie? Why not have it converted back into a barn? Then we can have a roll in the hay anytime.

She laughed and play punched his shoulder. He nuzzled her crown again, and then together they sank into an overstuffed settee. The flashlight dropped to a circle of braided rag carpet and rolled a few inches away, up against the leg of a coffee table. It was still on, but with the beam now pointing toward my own feet, encased like my brother's in bunion forgiving nylon and rubber.

All of a sudden, I was exhausted. And with the talk of barns and hay my ears and throat had begun to itch, though probably mold or mildew was the culprit: I could smell the dampness. I groped behind me and found a chair, dropping into what felt like down upholstery, a mistake if there were any actual feathers there, but I was too tired to care.

Lips and mouths made slick sounds, breath drew in and then out, but then, in less than a minute, it was over. My brother spoke, addressing me in the darkness over the coffee table, as if we'd all just been helping ourselves to sugar and cream:

She knows I could make her a better dark room in the estate house, with better light and climate control, once I get wiring and pipes put in, but she thinks this place has some kind of *animal energy*.

I do, Johnny, Grace said, still panting a little.

Now is this *clean* energy? Is it renewable or nonrenewable? I could hear the wink in my brother's voice.

Actually, you jerk, it's what I'd call *dirty* energy.

Oh, I like that.

I bet.

I was beginning to wheeze a little, when Grace started talking about animals, about how they, *especially the ones that don't eat meat*, were more connected to plants and *the primordial goop* before everything got *sorted out and divvied up*, and how horses, and cows, and even rabbits had *zillions of tiny organisms* inside them and passing through them all the time, in their shit, their piss, their spittle, slobber and drool, and as she went on to describe this waste that they excreted everywhere as *lavishly filthy*, as a *dirty energy* we humans refuse to recognize because we *fetishize form* and *hold on for dear life to what we already know*, I felt the constriction in my chest that heralds an asthmatic attack so that I'm not quite sure whether she said that in *our terror of this dirty energy* we *sanitize everything* or *fantasize* it, but I do know that I heard the phrase *allergic to reality*, as I jumped up and began stumbling toward my duffle bag, which I'd dropped by the door, to dig out the benadryl inside that it was maybe already too late to take but I would anyway because even though I very likely was *reality* averse, I did not want to die.

Struggling in the darkness to line up the little arrow on the childproof cap with the corresponding line on the bottleneck, even as my head had begun to spin and my vision to darken, I called in panic for the flashlight. I've got this, I heard Grace say. What happened next is a fog, a blurring of boundaries as I felt a rush, a beating in the air that might just as well been the throbbing of my veins, followed by a sense of seizure that could have come from within or without—I couldn't tell. The only thing I'm sure about was the sudden piercing jab in my thigh. Instantly my chest opened and my lungs filled but still I couldn't make out the features of the face looming over mine in the darkness even as I caught a tiny glimmer, a glint like a hovering firefly. No doubt it was Grace's diamond necklace, escaped from the neck of her collar and now dangling over my nose, while the piercing jab must've been the sting of an epipen. An epipen like the one Ormondo had saved me with back all those months ago when even though I was losing my friends I still knew who they were.

The evening ended there. Proclaiming in unison that I must be so tired, Grace and Johnny helped me to my feet. Grace had finally retrieved the flashlight and beamed a path to my room, which was behind the door to the right of the fireplace. As I stepped across the threshold, I looked back over my shoulder. In the window over the barn doors, the moon hung like a hex.

I fell asleep quickly, but then woke up again while it was still dark. Grace had left the flashlight, as well as a glass of red wine and some cheese, on the nightstand. I sat up and surveyed the room with the LED beam. The wall adjacent to the door was soot darkened brick, and partially recessed—the back of the fireplace, it appeared. Whoever had slept here—a horse, or maybe a stable boy— had been warmed by secondary heat seeping through the bricks. The ceiling was as high as in the common room on the other side, space enough for a barn swallow or a bat to fly up into, but not to flap around—the room was narrow like the stall it had presumably once been. On the other side of the room there was a window and also another door, leading to a bathroom, which tomorrow night, Grace told me, I'd be sharing with *one of the guys*. At least they didn't expect me to piss in the hay.

I drank some of the red wine. Then I pinched up a bit of cheese from the plate—a soft and crumbly goat cheese flavored strongly with the animal whose body had provided it. I tasted the glandular warmth of the mammary sac, the smooth dung imbued skin, and wished I could be young and thoughtless again. Or even to have someone young and thoughtless nuzzling against me, rooting in the dark—that would help counter the narrow nothing above. I took another morsel of cheese, then licked the crumbs from my fingers. The first one I didn't breast-feed—maybe it would've helped if I had, I don't know. But Kew I nursed until she was sixteen months, and only stopped because my milk dried up at a conference, during which I'd left her with her father (was that the last time I saw Adom? Yes, I think it was.). In fact, when I got back she ignored my breasts: once the milk was gone, it was like it never was.

We have one word here for her ladyship and her la dee da suck me not titties: *immunity.* Let alone the effect of them wee hormones on the heart. Course it would've helped.

Good for ye!

Eventually, sedated by the wine and the cheese, I slid back down into the pillows (which, by the way, were covered in fresh cotton pillowcases and seemed to be hypoallergenic. Unlike the rest of the contents of the carriage house, preserved in all their mildewed midcentury glory, the mattresses and bedding seemed new, and of good quality). Soon, I was falling back into sleep. But it was a descent like none I'd ever had before. As I fell, I shrank, my head (though not my awareness) diminishing until I no longer felt the support of the pillow, my limbs retracting, shriveling into tiny wires, my body collapsing and condensing within itself, growing smaller and smaller and smaller until I was no bigger than a beetle, buried in the massive bed. Panicking in that press of cotton from all sides, I rolled frantically about trying to find where bottom sheet and covers parted ways, so that now my tiny lungs were giving out.

When suddenly I began to grow again, expanding just as quickly as I'd contracted. Within seconds my head had pushed back out of the covers like a baby exiting its mother and in another moment the covers were resting on my ballooning belly like a washcloth and now I kept growing, getting bigger and bigger and bigger, my sides squashed up against the narrow walls my face pressing up against the ceiling so that once again I couldn't breathe at which point I opened my mouth to scream...

Out poured an animal stench the glandular heat of milk and piss and dung and with it I saw the ceiling recede, felt myself both deflating and contracting at the same time the space filled with the overpowering smell of an unmucked manger. Until finally I was back down on the bed again, the same size I'd been, as far as I could tell, before all this had started. But not the same texture. As I ran my hands over my arms to ascertain their dimensions, I felt fur glide beneath my palms—the soft slippery fur of a newborn foal or maybe a rabbit. I couldn't see the color and I sure as hell wasn't going to turn on the flashlight to check. I'd just wait to lose consciousness again, for surely these wonderland delusions were due to some cerebral malfunction (I remembered that Kevin occasionally used to suffer from "hypnagogic hallucinations"; maybe

I'd had one of those) and in the morning the fur on my arms would be gone.

And it was. I checked first thing in the dawn light filtering down through the pines outside into my bedroom window. Not only had the soft thick hair on my arms vanished, but also the air was clean again with the scent of coniferous sap. I took a few deep breaths and then I got up to use the bathroom. Only as I was sitting on the toilet did I look down and finally see the soft pelt, a silvery mouse brown, between my legs.

When I emerged a little while later from my bedroom, in a fresh t-shirt but the same soiled carhartts of yore, I'd put that little strip of fur out of mind. Probably the transformation had been happening for some time, and those fine soft hairs were the attenuated issue of aging follicles. I simply hadn't noticed.

There was no one in the big common room. But the barn doors, latched last night, had been slid wide open. Situated on the side of the house opposite the woods, they faced a great roll of misted lawn beyond which rose the hulk of the main house. I could smell wet mowed grass untainted at this hour by the sepulchral scent of Sunset Hall, and I understood why Grace preferred the carriage house. In early morning the interior walls, paneled wood painted a soft sage green, cradled the light—creating a sense of airy sanctuary.

I padded around, inspecting my new home. In addition to the salon-like clusters of mid century bourgeoisie—overstuffed couches and wing chairs paired with spindle legged coffee tables—there was, to the right of the front door, an old upright piano. I ran my fingers over the keys, testing the silence. Down at the opposite end of the room, a long painted wooden table with ladder back chairs providing seating for eight. I sat down in one and gazed over at the fireplace, behind which lay my strange stall. Above the zebra skin, which in the light of day looked fake (the borders of the ersatz hide were too regular), a great swathe of American flag bunting hung from the rafters. Who had put it there? Grace did not seem like the patriotic type, while my brother's only allegiance was to himself (and yet again I questioned the invitation that had brought me here. The crush he'd had on me as a kid was clearly over).

The sound of an engine revved in the distance. I stood up and walked over to the opening between the barn doors, and leaning out, peered round to the front of the house. Grace's SUV was still parked there, glistening with dew, and I idly wondered, hearing the faint noise of vehicular combustion, whether my brother still had a motorcycle. It was then, as I withdrew back into the house, that I noticed the wall of photographs, obscured in the shadows to the left of the doors. I walked over to take a look. Ranging in size from what I guessed to be twelve by fourteen inches to twice that, there were six of them. Next to a chaise lounge in the corner stood a lamp. I picked it up and brought it over, as close to the images as the outlet and cord would allow.

They were brilliant, and strangely, darkly hilarious. The subject matter, as far as I could tell, was animals. But the animals were visible only in bits and pieces, as fleeing parts and sallying slices, projecting hooves and receding muzzles, twisting flanks and turning udders, melting tails and shiny black debouching eyes, madly frolicking in and amongst pools of emulsion which, in turn, offered no visual purchase as these in some places had been teased out into swirling lines, that merged again to form planes, before disintegrating back into lines, and in other places had been scraped away entirely, to reveal the raw humor of the paper beneath. The effect was of incessant mutability and a comical disregard for the dictates of form. I thought of my hallucinatory dream the night before, as well as the body I was standing in right then and for a moment felt the accumulated caprice of the latter—that it was finally, a series of biological gaffes and material incompetencies hardened into a joke that was no longer funny. But maybe that was only because I took myself too seriously.

Good morning, Sunshine!

It was my brother, who had just walked through the screen door at the other end of the room. He was wearing a black motorcycle jacket and a helmet dangled from his hand. Evidently he did still have a bike, though his plume of silver hair appeared neither flattened by head gear nor tossed by wind.

I asked him whose work it was on the wall, though I'd already guessed the answer (and no, they weren't *crap* at all).

He came and stood beside me. I could smell his outdoorsy scent, which somehow smelled less convincing than the day before, despite his morning ride. Maybe it was just deodorant.

Grace did those. Weird, huh? But the photography keeps her busy. And she is getting some press, though nothing down in the city yet. They say that's a tough nut to crack.

Then he gripped my arm and turned me toward the

long table behind us: Take a load off, Sis. I'll get us some breakfast.

He disappeared through a door in the wall behind the table and reemerged a minute or two later with two bottles of probiotic drink and a plate with a few greasy looking golf ball-sized pastries. Handing me one of the bottles, he sat down and twisted off the cap on the other: Here's looking at you, kid.

He took a drink, belched: If you'd like to throw those farmer pants of yours in the wash later, feel free. I passed the NYSEG guys down the road—the power should be back on soon.

I set my bottle on the table, unopened. It was too early for lactobacillus, or maybe too late. I popped a pastry in my mouth, relishing the melt of crispy sugar and fat. Still chewing, I asked where Grace was.

Out taking pics. Pressing his palms together and pursing his lips, Johnny gave me an appraising look: we need to get you on a sugar and gluten free diet. Problem is that Grace is addicted to those donut holes and I don't eat breakfast myself.

He took another swig of the probiotic, then leaned back in his chair: But I'm glad to see you two getting along so well. Between you and me, she's a handful. As you might've noticed, she's a little high strung—the shaking, that crazy stuff about animal energy. Also, to put it delicately, a bit of a nympho. I think there's some hormonal thing going on—menopause or whatnot. She's older than she looks. But the photography distracts her, which gives me more time to work on the estate renovation. If it wasn't for that... His gaze drifted over in the direction of the mantel, then after a few moments, back to me:

Maybe you can talk to her about some of her ideas, which my friend Art, who used to be a professor over at the college, says aren't so out there as they sound. In fact, some of the stuff she says kind of reminds me of you and all your artsy friends, back in the day when I was just a hick kid from the western slopes of Colorado visiting my big sister in New York City.

He drained his drink and stood up: Well, I've gotta go meet another potential investor. Grace should be back soon, if you need anything.

Thanks, I said, reaching for another donut hole.

He caught my wrist: you really ought to try the probiotic.

Grace returned from *taking pics* shortly after my brother's second departure, looking flushed and sweaty, her camera slung around her neck, but she didn't stay around for long. I did try to engage her in a discussion about the photographs on the wall, not to shine her on as my brother had suggested (though I was beginning to comprehend my role: I was, it seemed, to be a kind of in-house intellectual pet, distracting and mollifying Grace with my mildly critical attentions), but because I thought her work was actually good. She seemed uninterested in discussing it, however. When I said that I thought she'd captured something of the essence of animals, she dismissed my comment:

Actually, what I'm trying to do is let them go.

Noting the Sally Mann book I'd picked up from a coffee table, she changed the subject: Mann's great but she's kind of a hoarder, ya know? Before I could ask her what she meant, she excused herself, saying that she needed to go upstairs and pull some prints out of the *bath*, and I returned to the Mann book (*The Flesh and the Spirit*, I think it was).

After that, I heard occasional sounds of creaking timbers from above, and wondered idly how she'd gotten up there, since there was no visible means of access in the common room—perhaps there was a staircase in one of the bedrooms. At midday, I took a too warm walk on the grounds, bypassing a path behind the carriage house leading into the woods, and discovered, at the far edge of the park, a cowshed connected to a fenced pasture where a couple of sleek brown cows grazed on wildflowers.

But mostly I just lazed around, leafing, after I'd finished with the Mann book, through the back issues of *Art Forum* that were scattered around the common room, making occasional forays into the old kitchen where I'd discovered a cupboard full of crackers (the donut holes were gone), and trying to ignore the slippery trickle between my legs (which had commenced mid morning, just a few hours after I first noticed the pelt). I assumed it was an infection of some sort, and stuffed the crotch of my underpants with toilet paper.

Johnny's friends arrived in the late afternoon. Johnny himself had returned only a short time before and was busy in the kitchen, while Grace was still hidden up in the loft, or wherever she was. I lay sprawled on a chaise lounge in the common room, looking at glossy photos of the Venice Biennale. With the whir and grind of the food processor, or maybe it was a juicer, in the next room (the power having at last been restored sometime in the early afternoon), I missed the slam of car doors and thump of feet. So suddenly there they were, two big men, framed by the slot of the open barn doors:

Bon Soir! bellowed the larger of the two, who was holding a white cardboard box.

As if on cue, the sounds in the kitchen ceased and Johnny popped out, wiping his hands on a white chef's apron: Welcome home, welcome home! Grace will be down soon.

And who is the lovely lady on the fainting couch? asked the man with the box, stepping into the house.

It had been almost thirty years since I'd last met any of Johnny's friends, the last time being when he and his buddy Travis (or possibly Gravis) had stopped on a cross-country bike trip to visit me in Denver. I was in graduate school and pregnant with Kew (though I didn't know it at the time). Travis or Gravis was long and levi lean, like all my brother's friends back then, with a bit of road stubble on his jaw and dirt under his fingernails. I didn't mind either, though after, the rash on my inner thighs and yeast infection in my cunt (which unlike the one I had now, benign but for the trickle, had itched and stung like hell) compromised my ability to sit through seminars for an entire week.

I stood up and walked over. The men were older, in their early sixties like my brother. My first thought was that the easy rider boys of yester year had been replaced by their dads, or granddads. But of course. Why was I surprised? We'd all been replaced, our original, streamlined on the road selves traded in for junkyard heaps.

Eyes a twinkle in his ruddy face, whiskey barrel torso

encased in clean denim carhartts (now I regretted not exchanging my own, still unlaundered, for the one remaining chicos piece in my duffle bag—a sand colored caftan), the taller man shifted one arm beneath the box and held out the other:

Hi, I'm Art Pelzmann.

Art squeezed my hand a moment too long, as if to press the matter of our shared shapes and apparel.

The prof here, Johnny said, used to teach college just like you, Sis. That really old Irish stuff from before people could read. And also the newer stuff that still nobody can read.

Art gave Johnny a light punch in the arm: Thanks, boyo. This is why since my retirement, I've devoted myself to my hobbies, farming and herbal medicine. My current products seem to have a much broader appeal than my books ever did.

Next was *Russell Finan*, squatter and tighter in the gut than Art, but thicker in the hips and thighs, who was a self-described *Hedgistan refugee enjoying the peace and quiet of upstate New York* in a pink golf shirt. As Russell loosely gripped my fingers, almost immediately letting go, a third much younger man with red lips and a close cropped but bushy blond beard appeared at the threshold behind him. The much younger man was holding what appeared to be a slim moleskin notebook in his hand, which he slid into his back pocket as he stepped forward.

This was Russell's son, *Tan the man*, as Johnny introduced him, or *Tanner* as he introduced himself. Recently graduated with a film studies major from a small private upstate college whose name I vaguely recognized as an educational refuge for the over privileged and under motivated where I might once have possibly applied for a job in the token women's studies program, Tanner had just *lucked into sales* with a new distillery in the touristy lakeside village where the bus had dropped me off. Hence he was *crashing at dad's country house* until he found a place of his own. Pectorals tautening a gray t-shirt printed with the word *CABO*, bullish thighs straining distressed levis, the kid was built like a rapist, but his grip was even limper than his father's. In fact, it was easy to imagine him transitioning into his father—there'd be no disjunct here between slim hipped youth and saddle bagged dad.

Johnny was in fact the most boyish of the four, the only one who still had a bounce to his step, cross trainers and all. As he bopped around, herding everyone out to the terrace that extended from the front of the carriage house, to a glass topped patio table already set with a bottle of tequila and an assortment of shot glasses, there was something adolescent in his manner, the air of an opportunistic teen taking advantage of his parents' weekend absence.

What's this rotgut? Russell demanded, lifting the tequila bottle.

That's a damn fine bourbon cask reposado Russ. Why are you knocking my booze?

Russell lowered his bulk into a chair: I know, Johnny Boy, I know. I'm just disappointed. I was looking forward to some more of Grace's red whammies. Mmm mmm, like velvet in the throat, those babies were.

And vegan too, said Tanner, settling catty corner to his father. Grace told me she uses chickpea water for the emulsifier.

Russell made a face: I don't believe it, a fine woman like that. Where the hell is she, anyway?

I'll go see what's keeping her, Johnny said. In the meantime, you all will just have to rough it.

Bring some dessert plates and forks, Art called after Johnny's retreating back.

Silence reigned, with Russell at the head of the table, Tanner to his right. I'd taken a seat on the left side of the table facing the front door, and Art had lowered himself into the seat next to mine, after placing the white cardboard box in the center of the table. Overhead, the porch light burned, even though there was still daylight—probably it had been on when the power went out and had come on again when it returned.

So what's in the box? I asked.

Love.

Come on.

No, seriously. *To try to write love is to confront the muck of language, that region of hysteria where language is both too much and too little.* So I've given up on that, but I like to think I've had some success with baking.

Art reached over and flipped back the lid of the box, revealing a pie. Purple red fruit filling oozed like sap from the slitted golden crust.

Russell sat back in his chair, folding his arms over his pink upholstered gut and closing his eyes. His son hunched over the table, jotting with a stub of pencil in the little notebook I'd spotted earlier. I turned my head and looked off in the direction of the estate house. A privet hedge grew along the back, perhaps to screen the windows from ogling stable boys.

Paper or plastic or both rustled beside me but I kept my gaze fixed on the privet hedge. Then a match struck and I smelled the acrid burn of cannabis.

Art nudged my shoulder: Want some?

I wasn't sure if he meant the pastry or the weed, but I shook my head, feigning indifference, even as I would've liked to try a bit of both, especially the latter. My greatest regret, leaving Colorado when I did, is that I will never enjoy the full legalization of marijuana.

Suit yourself.

I pushed back my chair and walked out from beneath the terrace roof into the last of the sun. It had been a cloudless day and in the late afternoon, the air remained dry and warm, even as the cool of evening seeped in, so that I could feel two temperatures at once, simultaneously. I passed the barn doors on the side of the carriage house. The tissue between my legs had grown soggy and I considered going inside to get a new clump before I rejoined the others. Or perhaps I would just retreat to my stall. But I didn't want to run into my brother, who would no doubt enlist me to carry drinks, or dips and chips, back to the jerks on the terrace. So I decided to wait before reentering the house and instead walked around to the rear of the building, along the edge of the woods.

Extending up the backside of the house to a door just beneath the gable of the roof, there was a wrought iron spiral staircase. So this was how the loft space above was accessed. As if to confirm my thought, the door opened. I slipped behind a pine. My brother stepped out onto the landing, sliding his wiry arms into his motorcycle jacket, shoving his shirt into his jeans. Gyring down the stairs, he called over his shoulder: The juice is on the counter princess, so all you have to do is make your magic.

A little while later, Grace stepped out. On the top half of her she wore the fisherman's sweater, but her long legged bottom half was bare. A pair of cargo pants were in her hand, and as I peered from behind my tree, she fished in the thigh pocket and pulled out a joint. For several minutes she stood there toking, scratching once or twice at the dark triangle of her crotch. Possibly she had parasites of some sort, but going on the indolence of her method, I guessed that she just liked the way the scratching felt. I noticed that the hand holding the joint was not shaking. Maybe sex had a steadying effect. When she finished the joint, she stubbed it against the side of the house and let it drop down to the ground. She lifted first one leg to the railing around the landing, then the other, touching her head to her knees. From below, I could see the dark pink slit between, glistening.

I waited until she'd put her pants on, descended and disappeared around the corner before I stepped from behind my tree. And then I waited some more before I finally started back around to join the others. But I no longer had any thoughts of returning to my stall, though the tissue between my legs was completely soaked.

Everyone was at the table now. And in my absence, it seemed as if a game of musical chairs had been played, though there was no music (thank god. As I recalled, my brother's taste inclined to rock anthems with long guitar solos). Grace sat at the end opposite Russell's chair, now vacant. Instead, Russell sat in the previously empty seat to her right, while Art had moved into what had been my seat, to her left. Johnny had taken Art's old place, while Tanner had remained where he was. All of the men were leaning in Grace's direction, except for my brother. Johnny, combing through his silver crest with his fingers, was genially observing Russell, who in turn seemed quite transformed. Lumpen silence a thing of the past, Russell gabbed and gesticulated at Grace, pausing only to take gulps of some thick and frothy red beverage.

As I sat down in Russell's former seat at the end of the table, Art picked up the blender pitcher sitting in the middle of the table and poured a tumbler full of the red drink, which he handed to Johnny to pass down to me. He did not cut me a slice of the pie, however, which was in any case almost gone—just a sliver remained in the tin in the white box. Small plates were scattered around the table, scraped clean except for a stray smear of purplish red jelly, here and there.

Russell was talking about aphrodisiacs—discoursing about his experiences with oysters and clams, deer antlers and rhinoceros horn, though he'd never tried Spanish fly because he couldn't bring himself to ingest something made from dried beetle dung (*that's just plain unsanitary*), at which point Grace interjected that shit was part of life and started on her dirt and animals spiel. All the men were transfixed except for Johnny, who nevertheless looked on with an appearance of paternalistic pride, as if Grace was his little girl, interviewing for a prize.

I tasted the drink. Gin was one of the predominant ingredients, but it took me a moment to identify the other, maybe because I'd been expecting tomato, as in a bloody mary. Only this was sweeter, darker and more acrid—the taste of earth rather than sun. I remembered the beets at Conrad's party and I took a big gulp, regurgitating my own descent. How far I'd fallen, and would fall. But there were other flavors as well—the wood mint taste of tarragon, and some spicier taste that I couldn't identify—flavors that put a spin on the beet, uprooted it and sent it whirling across a woodland glade or a warehouse floor. If I was falling, I could also pick myself up and dance. Fuck yeah.

I set my empty glass down on the table and instantly it seemed it was being refilled by Farmer Art who this time stood up and leaned in front of my brother, silently delivering the replenished drink to me himself. I mumbled a thank you, but he was already sitting back down again, his attention on Grace and the conversation at the end of the table.

I continued in my sink, appraising the man in profile. In his fleshy way, he wasn't bad looking. With a strong nose and long slightly slanting eye, the hint of a smile curving his lip, he looked a little like a statue of the Buddha—including the big paunch beneath his carhartt bib, pressing against the table. What would it look like, divested of its coverall? Like a big flabby roll or would it be the smooth muscled bloat of a football lineman or sumo wrestler? And what about the shoulders and back behind it, the length and strength required to hold that belly up? When he stood there was no stoop to him even though I guessed he was only a few years younger than me. Looking at him, I felt small, and even spry, although maybe that was the drink, already tasting like another, like an ongoing transfusion of vital new blood. What would it be like to clamber up on that big belly supporting back and spur the old goat on? What would it be like, when he stumbled, to bring us both down?

You liking those red whammies, Sis? Johnny grinned at me. I wondered if he'd caught me appraising Art. And if he had, what was he making of what he'd seen? Always looking for an angle, perhaps he now saw me horizontal beneath his hefty old friend, and was trying to calculate the value in that. Drunk as I was, it still added up to a sum I couldn't quite pocket.

They're refreshing, I replied, even as I felt a whisker of queasiness twitch in my gut. I put my glass down and whoozily tuned back into the conversation at the other end of the table, which had returned to aphrodisiacs, specifically plant-derived, with Tanner, who it seemed was quite the botanist, leading the discussion. Dismissing chocolate as *a candy factory fantasy* though *never underestimate the power of the placebo effect,* he detailed the effects of *natural medicinals* such as *damiana, muira puama* and *catuaba.*

Muira puama has a nice mood-lifting effect along with increased libido, Tanner said, pinching a bit of weed from the open baggie on the table, and tamping it down into a little brass pipe. While catuaba is more physiological, increasing blood flow. Some people like to mix them together—a best of both worlds deal. He stole a quick glance at Grace, his lips a rose bud in the bouquet of his blond beard.

Grace beckoned at the packed pipe, and Tanner stood up, waddling around his father's chair to hers, the thick thighs now looking more steer-like than bullish. Cupping the bowl with his hand, he lit it for her, continuing his discourse on medicinals:

I'm thinking you could make some kind of herbal liquor out if it—like the shit those monks make. Benedictine, chartreuse, troyanska slivova, what have you. Floated the idea by my boss the other day, suggested maybe they'd want to fly me down to Mexico or whatever to do some research.

Nice work kid, if you can get it, Russell approved.

Grace had taken a long toke from the pipe. Now she billowed out a cloud of smoke while at the same time stretching her arms upward, hands clasped, as she extended first one shoulder and then the other. Overhead, the fumes wove and unwove a ghostly extension of her cable knit sweater, banding and disbanding beneath the porch ceiling, coiling a cloud around the burning yellow bulb.

What about mushrooms? she asked, her voice husky from the smoke. A girlfriend of mine had some kind of mushroom and vodka mix at her cousin's wedding in Estonia. Everyone ended up in a meadow under the stars and it was like this hyperspace sex mode where you couldn't tell if it was you or somebody else.

Or a cow or a goat, Johnny cracked.

Fascinating, said Tanner. Handing the pipe to his father, he sat back in his seat and picked up his little moleskin notebook. Did your friend mention the name of the fungus she ingested?

No fungin idea what kind of fuckus it was. Whoa, that weed is really hittin' me. Grace fell back in her chair and took a deep breath.

Most likely fly agaric, offered Art. Scientifically known as Amanita muscaria. The name fly agaric supposedly derives from the practice of lacing bowls of milk with the dried, powdered form of the fungus, in order to draw flies. The flies become intoxicated, crash into walls and windows and die. But given the mushroom's psychoactive effects on humans, recorded since ancient times, it is also quite like that the name is connected to the Medieval belief that flies could enter a person's head and cause delusions. And in fact Amanita muscaria contains neurotoxins that can lead to sensory and somatic distortions such as synesthesia, macropsia and micropsia (aka Alice in Wonderland syndrome), attended by a sense of connection with the infinite, which is perhaps why Emily Dickinson describes hearing *a fly buzz when I died.*

Wow. Could you spell the scientific name? Tanner was scribbling away. Also, what do they look like?

A-m-a-n-i-t-a m-u-s-c-a-r-i-a, Art said, refilling the pipe with crumbled cannabis from the baggie on the table. I'm sure you've seen it in Victorian fairy tale illustrations or at least Super Mario graphics—the rosy red orange cap spotted with white, wart-like growths, the white stem and white gills—the iconic magic mushroom or toadstool. It emerges from the ground as a little white nub, quickly lengthening and looking, before the cap grows and spreads, like a phallus, as many mushrooms do. No doubt this phallic appearance has contributed to the association of mushrooms of all varieties with hanky panky in English, Irish and Western European mythologies—with fairy rings, orgiastic dancing, changeling illegitimacies and other elfin excesses. He paused to light the bowl, took a hit and exhaled.

I've been cultivating this strain for four years and I have to say that it's my best crop yet. It unwinds the mind and reweaves it with the body, restoring the logic of desire. But to get back to mushrooms, in a sense they are all phalluses, or more literally, penises. Or penises and vaginas combined—essentially the sex organs of the larger organism, which is all underground and can extend for hundreds of feet in all directions. In fact, calling the little capped stalk, or sporocarp, that you see in the grass a mushroom is like calling a penis a man.

Tanner giggled.

Speak for yourself, Art. Speak for yourself, Russell said. His arm was now circled around Grace, who looked completely stoned, her face blank as a Venus figurine.

Art passed the pipe and lighter to Johnny, who immediately handed them down to me.

So tell us Art, are mushrooms plants or animals? Johnny was leaning back in his chair, an indulgent smile on his face.

I pulled smoke down my throat, and felt it expand in my lungs.

I can answer that, Grace enunciated. They are neither, even though they share characteristics of both. The fucki are a kingdom unto themselves.

I have no clear memories of the night after that, or at least no connected or sequential memories. What I have are images and sensations, disjointed and isolated bits— seemingly untethered from any narrative context and yet perhaps held together by some subterranean mycelium. For what they're worth: A barn swallow or a bat. A beetle or a tiny, bitter ball of dung. A yellow light bulb and the taste of bile. A knocked over drink glass, blood red fanning over pebbled glass. A smooth cool toilet seat. A clump of tissue floating like a flower. A tiny slice of fruit pie cupped in a meaty palm. Licking. The taste of blueberries and butter on a bed of salty skin. The slip, slop, slide of something. Thick fingers on piano keys. Dancing. The slip, slop, slide of something. A crescent moon hanging like a hex. A stump or a root. A twisting ankle and a snaking tongue. Licking. A noseful of wet grass. The smell of mushrooms. A fat hard cock a slap happy ass and a slippery mouse. A rough wooden fence. The odor of manure. The slip, slop, slide of something. A big dark eye gleaming through a slit of stall door. Snort. A ladder. Bales of hay. A mouthful of hot horsey piss. A cuntfull, a cuntfull, a cuntfull. Soaked straw. Prickles. Sneezes. Big soft belly pressed to big soft belly. A slippery mouse. Licking. A sigh.

I assume you've already guessed, Madmaeve, where I woke up early the next morning, and maybe even with whom. The sun was just beginning to rise, soft gray light sifting through the window set just below the rafters of the cowshed roof. Heavy breathing moistened the nape of my neck. Grunting, lowing and snuffling sounds rose up from below. I lifted the meaty hand from my thigh and licked it. Salt and savory and still, faintly, the taste of fruit pastry. He stirred, gasped but didn't wake and I slid out from beneath the weight of his arm. I couldn't find my carhartts though he was still wearing his, the pink, surprisingly clean cap of his penis poking through the fly slit. The *sporocarp*, he'd called it.

Walking back to the cottage, I felt some tenderness in my ankle, but nothing more. If I'd twisted it, the damage was minor. I felt far better, in fact, than the amount of alcohol and whatever else I'd consumed would normally allow. Just a little queasy, that was all. And not the least bit itchy or congested, despite the night in the hay. My only problem was that I was naked from the waist down, my tee shirt just skimming the upper line of my pubic hair. I discovered my carhartts, though not my underpants, on the other side of the rise up from the shed—a heap of khaki lying in the wet grass like a cow patty. As I stepped into them, the image of Grace on the balcony came to mind—we'd both gone bottomless in the last twelve hours, though the look no doubt suited her better than me. Thank god for the sartorial assistance of darkness, I thought, as I gazed down at the flaccid roll of belly draped over my groin. Thank god I didn't have to see myself last night. Or him. And then I spotted the tuft of hair, or fur, peeking up from beneath the curve of flesh. My new pelt. That little silver brown merkin settled in the cleft of my thighs had entirely slipped my mind. Or had it? Hadn't I known it was there all along? Hadn't I *felt* it?

What was missing was the burning rawness I'd felt for days after the last time I attempted to accommodate a penis—the laceration of postmenopausal tissue, too thin and dry to meet the challenge of tumescence. The humiliating sting of it—there was none of that. Last night had been so easy, and in the course of things I'd taken the power of lubricity for granted. But now, in the light of day, I recognized the wonder of my new wetness. I touched the pelt, so slippery soft and felt something stir or turn inside.

I thought about going back to the cowshed but I'd almost reached the cottage, where my bed, with its excellent mattress, beckoned.

When I emerged from my bedroom several hours later, robed like a microfiber earth mother in my remaining piece of chicos, the sand toned caftan, my brother was sitting at the long table with the *Wall Street Journal* spread before him, his cell phone glowing in his hand, so absorbed in whatever he was reading that he seemed not to notice me. Russell was asleep, slack jawed and snoring, on the chaise lounge, catty corner to the wall of Grace's photographs. An issue of *Art Forum* lay face down on his stomach, a standing lamp burned overhead. His socks were on the floor, but otherwise he was fully clothed, still wearing the same pink shirt, now soiled with deep magenta splotches, from the night before. He looked like he needed a wife—someone to turn off the light and pick up the socks, and later to spray and launder the stained shirt. And I had no doubt he'd find one—rich men always do.

Johnny glanced up: Everyone's in the kitchen. Then he returned to his phone, but not before I'd seen the white exhaustion in his face.

Grace, Art and Tanner were all sitting around the kitchen table. Grace and Art were drinking coffee and eating donut holes, straight out of a grease-spotted white paper bag, while Tanner sat with his little moleskin notebook spread open on the formica surface, sipping from a tall green smoothie.

Pine filtered light fell through the panes of the back door at the other end of the room, illuminating their animated faces even as the roar of the water heater, a tall white cylinder in the corner, combined with the rumble of the sixties era dishwasher it presumably fueled, obscured what they were saying. There was something almost family-like, I thought, in their interaction, a sense of slapdash sociability, of slothful intimacy. Grace leaned forward with her chin resting on her palm, her half eaten donut hole dissolving in a puddle of coffee, oil slicked lips smiling serenely, uttering a few words here and there, as Art sat back in bodhisattva profile, one hand alternately plucking donut holes out of the bag and scratching at his belly, the other blessing the air as he explained, between mouthfuls, something to Tanner, who drank it all in, whatever they were saying, like mother's milk, intermittently giggling and nodding sagely, as he scribbled away in his notebook. Tanner's gray Cabo tee was, like his father's shirt, splotched with beet juice stains, but here they mingled with smoothie green, like tie-dye—a happy hippy accident. Looking on, I felt the vibe of an organic whole, a kind of grungy camaraderie the like of which I hadn't felt since the seventies, since my early days in the village when the collective energy had made me feel like I was bursting with talent, like a big ripe pimple of potential. All I needed, it had seemed back then, was to find my troupe, and my calling, whatever it was—writing, painting, performance—would be clear. But over the years, I'd lost it, whatever it was—the capacity to make art, or just the feeling that I could—especially after Belfast. And then I'd applied to graduate school.

Art caught sight of me standing in front of the door, and beckoned, patting the empty seat next to him. Then he returned his attention to Grace and Tanner, who were engaged in a discussion that as I sat down and the sounds of the appliances receded to the background, turned out to be about film, or more specifically, about making a film.

Well, said Grace, we've got the gun but we still need the girl. She'd pulled the necklace from out of the neckline of her fisherman sweater and was rolling the diamond between her fingertips so that it seemed to writhe, like an insect made of light.

I reached for a donut hole. As I stuffed it into my mouth, Grace turned to look at me appraisingly.

Obviously I can't be in it because I'm shooting and directing. Youse in, Sandra?

In what? I asked, licking my greasy fingers.

Tanner backtracked for my benefit: while we had all been off doing our *own thing* (and here Art reached under the table and squeezed my thigh), Tanner and his father had spent a good part of the night in stoned contemplation of Grace's photographs on the wall. At a certain point, the images had seemed to Tanner's dad *to take on a life of their own*, though he couldn't articulate what he meant by this, and had passed out shortly afterward. But after, dwelling on his father's utterance, Tanner had recalled a Godard quote from a film class: *Photography is truth. The cinema is truth twenty-four times per second.* What if Grace's images were to become animated? Not literally, because real animation would be *a pain in the ass*, but rather brought to life simply by putting Grace behind a digital camera? Because it'd still be *like Grace's eye was making all the decisions.* Right then and there he'd jotted all this down in his little moleskin notebook under the headline *GET GRACE TO MAKE A MOVIE!*

With a sense of temerity, Tanner showed the notebook to Grace the next morning: I was afraid she was going to tell me to fuck off, but she loved the idea. However, unlike photographs, Grace had reminded him, *movies need a beginning, middle and an end, if not in that order.* So what was Grace's movie gonna be about? That was a tough one because as Grace had put it, *I don't think much about stories.* Grace being *pretty much anti-narrative.* Like she was *not even interested in images, in the traditional sense.* Then Art, who'd gone to town to buy donuts and a newspaper, had walked in.

This guy knows everything about narrative and anti-narrative—he even wrote a book about it: *The Subversion of Storytelling.* Right, Art? With Art's help, a brain storming session had ensued, and what the three had come up with was *a story that wasn't too much of a story* that would draw on Grace's current favored subjects, cows and rabbits, because *they're there, ya know?* and Godard's famous assertion that *all you need for a movie is a gun and girl.*

The basis of the tale, it seemed, was an appropriation of an old northern Irish yarn Art knew about a milk siphoning female *were hare* who nightly drains a poor farmer's dairy cows, until finally, the farmer's hired hand executes ballistic justice, revealing that the hare is actually the wife of a neighbor farmer, whose cows have been suspiciously productive. But that, Tanner said, was neither here nor there:

The setting could just as easily be upstate New York. I mean you've got the same elements: farming, wildlife, poverty and easy access to firearms.

With the phrase *easy access to firearms*, the din of the water heater and dishwasher suddenly ceased. Out in the common room, through the open kitchen door, my brother's voice rose:

That shit you told me to buy, it's been tanking for the last hour!

Jesus, Johnny, I was trying to sleep. Things go up and they go down. That's the way life is.

Castles in the air, castles in the air! All of it! Listen to this! Then Johnny read off a string of names and figures that might as well have been Gaelic.

Russell mumbled something inaudible.

That's all you can say—*that's too bad?* I am wiped out, completely annihilated, you hear me?!

Listen, if this continues, I'm going to be hurting, too. Probably I won't be able to invest in your sunrise or sunset or whatever the sunny hell it was deal.

You won't be able to invest? Fuck you. You misrepresented those IPOs—you said they were solid gold. You owe me.

First, I would never make a jackass statement like that. Second, I don't owe you anything more than you owe me. You want to talk about misrepresentation? What about that hag sister of yours?

That was when Grace jumped up and yelled: Enough already!

Then she strode from the kitchen out into the common room: If it's gone, Johnny, it's gone. It was my money anyway and I don't wanna hear about it. You're both gonna be in my movie, and that's that.

Once again, I should have left right then. I don't know why I stayed. The red whammies, the killer weed, the bad stock tips and amateur theatrics, not to mention the hag and the gun—it was not going to end well. And then there was that soft little pelt, the queer trickle between my legs like a portent of catastrophe. What kept me there? Curiosity, maybe. But let's not underestimate the power of the dramatic imperative. The show must go on, whether we like it or not.

Back in the day, I took part in a couple of performance pieces. I was in fact an animal in Simone Forti's zoological dance extravaganza *Planet* at PS 1 in the late seventies, before we left for Belfast, though I don't remember exactly what kind. Something small and non-predatory, I think. But I had never been in a play, after grade school, and certainly never in a film. Most of the day I sat around, waiting for the fun to begin, leaving the carriage house only once to drive to the Price Chopper in Richfield Springs with Art, where I bought a box of maxi pads (the toilet tissue was getting old). In the meantime, the others gathered props and costumes, scouted potential settings, and performed color and *skin tone* tests with Tanner's expensive looking digital movie camera. Grace decided that the film would be shot in three different locations—*the dairy farm* (the cowshed and environs), *the countryside* (the general grounds of the estate), and *fireside at the farmhouse* (the area in front of the fireplace at the cottage). I can tell you now that we never made it to the last location.

There was no script, or even a synopsis, just a cast of characters and some *production notes*, dictated by Grace, which Tanner had jotted down in his moleskin notebook. Dialogue would be *improvised*, while direction would occur on the fly, with Art standing by as *story consultant*. At some point, Tanner distributed copies of his notebook page, which he'd photocopied while picking up his camera from his father's house. I still have mine, blood stained but legible, here transcribed:

Title: To be determined
Setting: Rural upstate New York, sometime in the past
Story consultant: Art
Notes: The rabbit is just a rabbit. The woman is just a woman. No special effects. Hand held camera, cinéma vérité method. As much as possible, the camera will be unobtrusive and subjects will be encouraged to behave as if it isn't there. However, the camera is a catalyst and does provoke reactions.

Farmer 1: Johnny
Farmer 2: Russell
Hired Hand: Tanner
Woman: Sandra
Rabbit: rabbit
Cows: cows
Were hare: ?

I have not seen the film that Grace made, if one even exists. At any rate, I'm sure it would provide no clear picture of the night's events, given its maker's disinterest in narrative as well as her shaking hands. So all I have to draw on here is my own subjective experience. Nothing more, that is, than I have had all along.

We began with a round of red whammies, served again on the terrace. *To loosen up*, Grace said. Russell, Johnny and Tanner were all wearing carhartts, borrowed from Art, which fit the two larger men reasonably well, especially Russell, but sagged on my brother, making him look small and shrunken. A drink in his right hand, he cradled the old rifle that had hung above the mantel in the crook of his left arm.

You check to make sure there's no ammo in that? Russell asked.

Course. You think I'm an eejit? He slugged the rest of his drink, then slammed it down on the glass. You know, I'm fucking sick of beet juice.

Then don't drink it, Johnny, Grace said.

After some thought, Grace had decided I should wear my chicos caftan, with a piece of robe tied around my waist, since this would help to *visually separate* me from the men. It also aided in concealing the bump of maxi pad protruding from beneath the cleft of my buttocks like the beginning of a tail.

When the pitcher of whammies was finished, we all trooped over the grounds down to the cowshed, which I learned contained, in addition to the cows, hutched rabbits (somehow the bunnies had escaped my notice during my last visit). Both, Johnny informed us, belonged to a neighbor who raised the first for milk and the second for meat. This neighbor used the shed and pasture for *practically nothing* since Grace wouldn't raise the rent.

Because we don't need the money, Johnny.

We do now, Grace.

I leaned back into Art's big soft gut, chewing on a stalk

of queen anne's lace, and watched Grace release a large ash gray rabbit into the grass outside the shed. Then, as Tanner coaxed it along with a few limp beet greens, she filmed it reentering through the conveniently open door.

Good rabbit, ignore that camera, I said.

I know you were commenting on the artifice of the situation, but actually, that was cinéma vérité at its most convincing. Art passed me a lighted joint. In fact, the animal *always* ignores the camera. At most its gaze flickers and passes on. They look sideways. They look blindly beyond...

The sun was descending, diffusing the horizon with a tissuey pink. Grace and Tanner were conferring outside the cowshed about the results of Tanner's earlier *low light test* and what camera adjustments would be required in the dim interior. My brother was sitting back against the wood siding, the rifle across his lap, basking in the late afternoon rays. Russell had strolled off into the meadow, a rosie blob floating in the tall grass. Art wrapped his arm around me, pulling me into the warm billow of his body.

I felt, for the first time in a very long while, contentment. Contentment. Not the satiation of sex, even though it had been ages, before last night, since I'd felt that too. For years and years I'd been at loose ends, my whole life maybe though there had been connections here and there, one or two even, like Kew, that should have been lasting bonds but even at that time must have felt severable. Otherwise I would've done differently. The hard truth was that I had never committed myself to anyone or anything—not to poetry or painting, or whatever the fuck I thought I was doing back in the seventies and eighties, not to scholarship despite or because of my ill-begotten Ph.D, not to parenthood, though I'd had two chances at it. And maybe it was too late for com- **Two too bleedin many.** mitment: I knew my ties to these people, to this place, to be tenuous at best. But that didn't mean I couldn't enjoy this sense of happy belonging, like a pet snuggled in its master's arms. All I needed to do was to dedicate myself to my new role.

Inside the shed, a shaft of light slanted through the window in the loft, illuminating a loose puddle of beige nylon by the foot of the ladder. My missing underwear. I stooped to pick them up, then realized I had no pocket in the caftan in which to stash them. So I toed them beneath a loose pile of straw. It was uncomfortably warm, no doubt due to the combined effect of the sun beating down on the roof all day and the body heat generated by the animals. I pushed up the loose sleeves of the caftan to cool myself, and that's when I saw the hair, or fur, the same as in my room that first night—soft brushy gray sheathing my arms from the shoulders to the wrists. I yanked my sleeves back down. And then Grace was summoning me over to one of the two cow stalls, the slatted metal gate open and filled by the cow's simultaneously full and bony backside, tail swishing its shit besmeared flanks.

Don't worry, Shirley won't kick. I photograph her all the time and she's a real sweetie.

Grace guided me into the stall, alongside the animal and then underneath, gently pushing on my head. I felt like a child being coerced into a bath. A filthy bath of dung and old hay and sour mash, though oddly, there was no smell of milk, fresh or otherwise. I wondered why not and realized that I knew nothing about cows. Growing up, the only animals I'd known, besides my father's hunting dogs, were dead ones—the deer he shot each fall, and once on a trip to Tennessee or maybe Texas, a boar. I reached up and touched the pendulous pinky white sac, so finely hirsute, fingered one of the four squishy black teats. Then I heard something rustle and snort and threw myself against the wall, afraid of being kicked. But it was only the cow in the adjoining stall. I settled back down on my haunches.

That was great, I heard Tanner say. So convincingly skittish. I was doing some research on hares this afternoon. They're actually faster in proportion to their size than cheetahs—37 body lengths a second versus 23.

Okay now Sandra, make as if you're having a wee drink, Art instructed in an Irish accent.

Wait a fuckin' minute, Johnny's voice, sounding slurred, broke in. Innit spose to be my fuckin' cow?

I touched my lips to the teat. It was warm and dry and I couldn't taste anything but flesh, which despite the fecal tang, could've been human. My stomach rumbled—I'd had nothing but donut holes since the morning and suddenly I found myself wanting only warm milk. I put a hand on either side of the teat, rolled it between them, kneading and squeezing. And I sucked as hard as I could, but still nothing came, even as I heard my brother grumbling in the background about how once again he was gettin' fleeced.

When suddenly my mouth was filling—filling with warm sweet milk. I swallowed and kept kneading and sucking though I really didn't need to do either any-more—the milk just flowed. Mouthful after mouthful so that I felt my belly filling and then swelling like a water balloon and I knew that if I didn't stop soon I wouldn't be able to run and so finally I tore my lips away, wiping my mouth with my paw.

Then the light was on me, a flashlight beam and the camera as well, and I could see all of them out of the side of my head, Grace and Art and Tanner, and Russell looking bored and disgruntled behind them and Johnny yelling and waving the rifle at Tanner but I couldn't understand a word, I was oh so scared my heart swelling and filling the cavity of my chest as simultaneously my belly shrank and piss gushed down between my legs. And then I bolted—out of the stall across the shed through the open door in what felt like a single bound and I was running over the ground with great soft strides up the rise from the shed and down again, the wind rippling my pelt drinking in the moist now night air watching the land slide behind me, the tree line of the woods on one side, the rolling lawn on the other like I was a speeding train and my eyes were the windows and I could see out on both sides at once exulting in the power of my long strong legs flipping them all off with my white flap of a tail even as my newly sharp ears and nose told me I hadn't lost them yet, so that I redoubled my efforts when suddenly I hit something and I felt myself fly head over heels, and falling, catch my back left leg in a rut or a hole, the same one I'd twisted the night before, before I tumbled to a stop.

And now I was hobbled, maybe only temporarily, but I was losing my advantage. Behind me all I could see was the fallen tree, probably from the recent storm, that I'd somersaulted over, but I could hear the din, the menace of their voices. For a moment I felt myself frozen but then my eye caught sight of the dark hulk of Sunset Hall looming up ahead and I remembered what Johnny had said about fifty rooms. And I thought how they'd never find me—I would live out my days scampering through the vast maze inside.

A gust of spoiled meat mixed with synthesized meadow flowers filled my nose and I knew it was Johnny. Nostrils trembling, I pulled myself up, limp hopped along as I fast as I could to the estate house, toward the huge portico that led to the front entrance. I could smell them, hear them, and now even see them, though I didn't turn to look—with my sideways vision it was almost as if I had eyes in the back of my head. And what I saw was a monstrous moving clump composed of bipeds with tentacled paws and gaping mouths emitting sounds as undifferentiated as their bodies—so that the only way I could pick them out from one another was by their smells. Art's more like smoked meat than spoiled like ham mixed with rock candy like an old country store and the vinegary smell of the dark room mixed with sex that I knew was Grace's, but I couldn't tell how these smells, jumbled with the others, related to my situation. What did smoked ham, crystallized sugar and photo developing chemicals have to do with me? So I kept on hopping and stumbling, scrambling finally up the steps onto the surface of the portico, skittering across the smooth stone until at last I reached the big black painted door. Stretching, I grasped the brass knob and turned.

The shot was so loud that for several moments after I couldn't hear anything. All that registered was the blistering pain in my left thigh. Then suddenly they were all talking, voices once again distinguishable one from the other and comprehensible as well.

What the fuck, Johnny! Russell yelled, outrage laced with glee.

Actually, I think that was me when I tried to get the gun away from him, Grace said matter-of-factly.

I felt her wrapping some rough textured thing around my thigh. Through slitted eyes I saw that she'd pulled off her sweater and was now tying it into a makeshift tourniquet.

She's in shock, Art said. We need to get her some blankets and then to the hospital.

I'll go get them and come back with my dad's car. I was a division two sprinter in high school, believe it or not, Tanner said. Man, I'm so glad that wasn't me holding the gun. Who would've known it was loaded?

My final memory of the night is of being hoisted into the back seat of Russell's SUV, wrapped in the ersatz zebra rug that had hung over the fireplace (it was the first thing I saw, Tanner said), by Grace, Art and Tanner. I have no clear recollection of the next day, though it turned out that I wasn't so badly hurt: the bullet had missed major arteries, muscle and bone, rendering my wound *superficial* and hospital convalescence unnecessary (or maybe it was my crappy insurance that did that). Art came to visit me in my bed at Grace's, I think, offering me his spare bedroom to recover in, and perhaps I said I'd consider his proposal, though it is also possible that I pretended to be asleep. I am certain though that Johnny came in at some point with my carhartts, freshly laundered, because when I woke up the next morning, two days after the shooting, they were still there, neatly folded on the end of the bed with one hundred dollars tucked inside the bib. By then Johnny himself was already gone.

Grace shrugged Johnny's departure off: *No big loss.* Sure my brother's speculations had cleaned her out, compelling the sale of Sunset Park, which went on the market within the week. But she soon regained domestic equilibrium with the help of her trader sister, Antoinette, A.K.A. "Tony." Not only does Tony own a two-bedroom loft in Chelsea, just blocks away from a gallery that recently offered Grace representation, but the other day she closed on the old atelier above the loft, which will serve as studio and dark room space for Grace.

It is a purchase that, unfortunately, negatively impacts my own current housing arrangement, this storage room where I have been residing for the past three months. Obviously, once Grace has moved her belongings to the atelier she will no longer be able to justify the monthly rental expense to Tony. Nor can I afford to assume it myself—this is lower Manhattan after all. When Grace called this morning to ask me what I'm *gonna do*, I could hear Tony in the background:

Tell her there's loads of affordable senior housing in Newark.

I've written above that I have no clear recollection of the day after I was shot: what I meant was of that actual day. But as I lay there, drifting in and out of consciousness, floating on a raft of vicodin (all gone now, alas), another day materialized out of the mist. It was a day not unlike the one I was currently in. Then, as now, I was in bed and in pain that prescription painkillers dulled but could not cure, even as they robbed me of focus. I couldn't read, I couldn't even really think—my thoughts eddying round and round in my mind. Would I get tenure? Would I get tenure? Would I get tenure? And what would happen if I didn't? I could not even go there.

My bed was on the top floor of our one hundred-year-old Denver square, a splendid wreck of a house that I'd bought with the help of the university's faculty housing assistance program, shortly after I'd been hired, in a neighborhood slowly but sedately gentrifying. There were two large rooms and a small bathroom tucked up there under the eaves, one of which I used as a bedroom, and the other as a study, and windows all around, and if I sat up in my bed I had an even better view of downtown Denver than Konrad and Ormondo. But that day I couldn't sit up without pulling at the stitches from my recent hysterectomy. And there was nothing to look at but a copy of my manuscript on the desk, visible through the door between the two rooms, which had only been accepted for publication a week before, a full month past the university's deadline, plus I'd pissed off a full professor as well as an associate, both of whom would be voting on my tenure case, by becoming entangled with the latter (I won't unknot that affair here).

Kew and the current graduate student slash companion/babysitter for Kew slash sometime lover for me had their bedrooms below, on the second floor, though it was spring break and the graduate student (Carla or Marla), was out of town. For the first time I regretted the bedroom arrangement. The mere sound of footsteps in the hall outside the door, the flush of a toilet through the wall, would've penetrated the wadding of medicated pain, and maybe even brought the welcome wince of a visitor plopping on the bed. But from the beginning, since she could first climb stairs, I'd discouraged Kew from coming up: *Mama's working (or fucking)*. Now that I was incapable of doing either, it seemed that I'd trained her too well.

And then I heard the creak of the door at the bottom of the stairwell (my ears were better then). For a few seconds all was a hush and I held my breath straining for feet striking bare wood and then they did, a steady upwards thumping. At the top, Kew emerged holding a Gameboy in one hand and a glass of orange juice in the other:

I brought you something to drink.

She didn't look at me as she set the glass down on a coaster on the bedside table. She never looked at me anymore. I dropped my eyes from her closed off face to her legs. One was bruised deep purple above the knee, and I wondered how she'd hurt herself, my cat-like Kew who even as a toddler had never tripped or fallen. Once or twice from my third floor window I'd seen her skateboarding down in the parking lot of the check cashing business next door, and paused to watch, arrested by her balance. Which could perhaps be attributed to her long strong feet, already two sizes larger than my own, now planted beside my bed.

She seemed to hesitate and I imagined her gracefully twisting and folding her body down onto the bed, her beautiful feet firmly anchored to the floor, even dreaded the pain I'd feel if she sat down too hard like I'd once anticipated the letdown of milk into my breasts. But of course that didn't happen. Instead she walked away, slouching down into the little upholstered chair in the corner (site of many a head session, both given and received).

She bent over the Gameboy, pressing its little buttons, and for a while I dozed in the sunlight falling through the window above the bed. But at a certain point the sun became too strong, as it tends to in the west (even in early spring), and I opened my eyes. Before I could even hoist myself up on my elbows to turn and pull the shade cord, Kew was there, dropping the shade for me. I thanked her. She asked me if I'd like her to fluff the pillows behind my back and I said yes. Then she asked if I was feeling hungry and even though I wasn't, I said yes again. She went downstairs and came up a little while later with a tray: more juice and a little plastic container of applesauce and toast broken by the hard butter she'd attempted to spread it with. There was even a chrysanthemum in a jelly jar, plucked it appeared, from the bouquet I'd received in the hospital from three graduate students who'd recently asked for recommendation letters. And so it continued through the afternoon, Kew nursing me as I in turn fed on her attention. We even spoke a little, and I affected fascination when she told me about her favorite video game, *Legend of Zelda: Ocarina of Time* and why she loved it so much (*for the music*), just to keep her talking. I always liked her voice, the sane and level sweetness of it, just a little droning—even when it broke, the steadiness remained. As I started to drift off, I promised myself that when I woke up, I'd listen to her more.

I opened my eyes again to dusk and the empty upholstered chair. And then through the open doorway came the sound of rustling in the other room. I eased myself up and squinted (this was before my laser surgery): I could see her at my desk at the end of the other room, holding a sheaf of papers that appeared to be from my manuscript in her hands.

I'd like to blame the nineties for my books, the first of which got me my job, the second tenure. And the eighties too, since that is when I began the first one. There was a shift in academic writing around that time, which may have even begun back in the seventies, before I ever considered going to graduate school. The *C'est Moi Movement*, I'll call it, since it was the French who conceived it, though American feminists carried it. Objectivity was a fiction, post-structuralist theory declared, so might as well get your *I* on. Suddenly no academic essay was complete without the autobiographical first person jumping out of the prose like the girl out of the cake. But the fact is that I went way beyond that, even as I buttressed my prose—buttressed and girded and bulwarked and armored my prose—in pages and pages of research and footnotes and bibliography, to the point where it was practically impregnable, as well as inedible. For you see there was not just one girl in my books, but two, even though my daughter was born a biological boy.

I'd like to blame the nineties and the eighties, and maybe the seventies as well. But finally the fault is entirely mine. Instead of acknowledging my puny imagination

I embraced it, as if ego could make up for the inability to transform me into *not-me*. Or as an old lover, a rather good painter, once said to me, quoting Kim Gordon, *you're never going anywhere.* Of course I could have tried to at least be a good academic and found, through diligent research, something to write about besides my experience as a white woman giving birth to a mixed race baby boy in a racist and sexist culture (book number one) or my experience raising a mixed race baby boy who at age three decided he was a she in a racist and sexist culture (book number two), but I was too busy screwing around.

A year later, Kew went to live with her father, who was back in New York, working for Sloan Kettering. There was no scene—there was never any scene—but when I asked her why she was leaving, she said, *You acted like I was just there for you. Like you could do whatever you wanted with me. Make me into shoes for your feet. Or a fur hat for your head.*

And she was right, though I had never intended to make her into anything other than herself. I hadn't in fact intended to make her at all. I remember the first time I held her in my arms, when she was

Tis enough to make ye boke. First off, tis "way too late" for that. The sapless aul bitch hasn't nary a drop left in her. Second, she had years to make it up to ye— years. She coulda tracked ye down, if she really wanted to, covered that *quare* distance, if she'd cared to. So don't be lettin' her play ye or make ye again into mammy's wee craytur (aka a fur toque for her high and mighty head).

Ach, we know tis hard for ye to resist, hard not to buckle when ye haven't anyone to hold on to. We did some research on yousuns. Dr. Adom Kambi is surely up to his gills as chief of Human Oncology and Pathogenesis at Sloan Kettering and begetter of three children under the age of five with his fellow begetter and gogetter, the lovely Dr. Natalie Kambi, who though thirty years younger than yer da (begob, only four years older than ye!), is already at the top of her own medical field: hematology. Even if it weren't for Dr. Natalie's inexplicably bilious disposition (for what has the woman to complain about?), yer da thought it best to set ye up in yer own place out in Queens. Tis a long way into the city... And though yer da sends you a monthly allowance to supplement yer pitiful Petsmart salary, money can't buy ye a life.

At twenty-six years of age, ye still haven't found yer niche, have ye? School wasn't for ye and the only things ye were ever really any good at were skate boardin and video games. Ye think ye might get into "music" or perform in poetry slams though ye've never learned to play anything but the recorder and ye've never memorized anything but the lyrics to "Robots in Disguise": "Something evil's watching over you/Comin' from the sky above/There's nothin' you can do" (clearly ye saw bad attention as better than no attention a'tall), let alone written a word of yer own. Which is not to say ye don't have potential. Look at yer feet: they're longfellows. Hee hee.

The only thing ye've ever managed to practice on a regular basis is safe sex. And to be sure, ye do have some success there, with both the girleens and the boyos (for yer ye mammy's child, joystick, jubilee button and all). But it never lasts. "I'm too fucked up," ye always tell them when the fun is done—"too fucked up to be with anyone."

still newly *him*, having been for months *it*, the gender neutral spawn of maternal ambivalence, conceived in the erotic murk of my relationship with Adom (twice I'd scheduled and cancelled abortions). How, I wondered, could something so small, and suddenly so light (minus the fifteen vein popping pounds of fluid and placenta), generate such an immensity of feeling, such tremendous gratitude? *This is for me,* I thought, after everything squandered (including the one before, my first baby boy, my abortion three months after the fact). *This is a gift that I will treasure and keep.* Ha, because if I don't laugh I will cry.

So what now, Madmaeve, though of course, as usual, I won't subject you to any of this long tale of senile folly and self-sabotage. All you will receive is the message I sent yesterday, availing myself of the free wifi at the street level coffee shop next door. It was the customary digital yelp, a fakebook cour de cri, howled in emojis because words are TMI: house icon (less) + gun icon + smiley face with bandage icon. With a couple of screw

Aye, tis true that yer fucked up. Right now yer like some broken winged thing, too mangled to fly. Banjaxed and bollixed in yer wee Queen's cage, ye feel like yer trapped. Yet oh if ye were fixed, ye would surely be flittin all around, turning somersaults in the air, skimmin and flippin and soarin like ye were born to it. Well we can do that:

fix ye up and kit you out.

And you will be happy down here with us, so happy— we're like a family without all the familial bullshite. To be sure, tis always a wee bit cold, but you will hardly notice, after a while. If we're shiverin right now, we assure you all the feckin ecstasy is what does it.

icons thrown in though I did, all in all, enjoy it. My intention being to capture your feeble feminista interest without exhausting it. So that when I hobble downstairs again later, perhaps you'll have written back. For I do so love your bland, trivializing little replies, your anemic solace. Which is in a way helpful—a reminder that it all drains away in the end, whether we slit our wrists or not.

On Weds, Jan 8th, 2014 at 12:10am, Madmaeve <madmaeve17@gmail> wrote:
Don't despair. Surely there's hope for ye yet.

If hope, Kevin once said to me after a particularly vicious fight, *is the thing with feathers that perches in the soul, what's in you is a durty stinkin pigeon.*

So what to make of the message I found a little while ago, just a few lines down from yours, embedded in a stack of junk mail from mortgage refinancers, planned parenthood and amnesty international solicitors and diet pill purveyors, from a certain Jeanine Malarkey, Professor of Sociology and Director of the Queer Studies Program at Queen's University Belfast, offering me a lectureship for the spring semester. *One of our full time instructors will be on maternity leave, and hence we need to find a replacement. You were recommended to me by a colleague who was much impressed by your Confounding Boundaries: Race, Gender and Identity in an American Family,* she wrote, or some such. And then *we can offer an advance as well as travel expenses.*

It's got to be a scam, a durty stinkin pigeon, or maybe just a bat in the belfry, though I not only read the message three times, but asked the young woman at the next table, multiply pierced but otherwise imperviously sane looking, to read it aloud for me. Wow, she said. Lucky you. I'd love to go to Northern Ireland and see all those *Game of Thrones* places.

I haven't watched the show she was referring to—fantasy has never been my thing. But the reality is that I have no other options. And it's been thirty-five years since I was in Belfast—at least two generations of Killeens, maybe even three (one of the sisters, I recall, had her first baby at age sixteen). Whatever bad feelings I left behind me have no doubt faded, like all stinks do.

So sure, there's hope for me yet, Madmaeve, why not? Not to mention the opportunity to meet you. Once I make flight arrangements, I'll let you know the date and time of my arrival, so you can meet me at the airport with a big placard: *Fáilte, Sandra Dorn!* Just kidding, but I do hope we can get together once I've settled in.

I'm writing though I haven't had a word from you, Madmaeve, since my arrival. Writing though I've been in Belfast for almost a month and surely if you were interested in meeting me, you would have sent me an email by now, or perhaps a text, using the number I dispatched to you as soon as I got my new iPhone (my credit magically restored by Queen's University Human Resources). For now that there's no longer an ocean between us, digital silence is the only means of division. One response from you would encourage me to solicit another, and another, and another, each attempt to close the virtual gap bringing me closer to getting my bunioned foot in your door, literally. Having foreseen this horror, you've chosen to avoid it, by ceasing to communicate with me altogether.

A horror that, regrettably, I helped you envision: I should not have accompanied my phone number with a selfie. Digital photography is no flatterer of the old, no matter how you filter it. I went with *noir* (better shady than shutterstock *elderly lady*), which did no favors for me or my new threads, a Liberty print button down patterned with peacock feathers and a tailored suit of silk threaded green wool, all commissioned from the bespoke menswear shop on the Lisburn Road. Somehow the light setting turned rich and lustrous to cheap and lurid. Or maybe that was the veil of cigarette smoke, obscuring the weave and distorting the lines (I've been smoking like a fiend since I got back here).

At the same time, it doesn't seem quite fair, now that you know what I look like, to give me no opportunity to similarly spot you. You could, for instance, be here in this cafe just a few blocks from the University, where I've been sitting now for hours, drinking sugary tea, dipping now and then into a volume of *Door Into the Dark* that I found on the bookshelf in my flat, watching the student patrons come and go, tuning in and out of conversations with ears that since the incident at Grace's house have grown supernaturally acute. Conversations about grades and profs and parties, the daily froth of life within the collegiate bubble, except for one exchange about the bomb that went off last night in the City Cemetery. That, I must say, was not in the reckoning. Malarkey assured me in her email that the Troubles were long over. *You will be pleased to see what a vibrant, cosmopolitan, and peaceable city Belfast has become.*

Perhaps that's you with your back to me by the far window gazing out at the gate of the Botanic Gardens, stirring a pencil in a mass of red curls. The only young woman in the cafe without a straight blow out—that would have to be you, going on your tweet several weeks ago about Belfast's *fake baked, sheet haired sheep*, who've *processed the thoughts right out of their heads* (which come to think of it predated my arrival; you seem to have taken a hiatus from social media, as well as to have ceased attending to your blog). That would have to be you, if you were here. But I imagine that you're not.

Then again, why not imagine that you are, since more and more I seem to be imagining things, peopling a world that I'm beginning to suspect exists only for me (last night's cemetery bomb notwithstanding). What happened the other day, for instance, as I met with my first class. I assume you have some acquaintance with Queen's University, just a stone's throw beyond the Botanic Gardens, though when I lived in Belfast with Kevin, we never ventured there (a bunch of Earl Grey slurping poufers full up with royal piss, he used to call them, though his favorite poet was an alumni; I wonder what Kevin would think of the since established Seamus Heaney Centre). Perhaps you've even taken a course or two in one of the row of Victorian townhouses on University Square that contain the various Humanities departments—English literature, History, Philosophy and Political Science, Film Studies (about which the Queer Studies Program seems to flit, an interdisciplinary fairy housed everywhere and nowhere). My classroom is at the top of one of these, a garret accessible only by three narrow flights of stairs.

A few hours before class, I'd received an email apology

from Professor Malarkey (whom I've yet to meet) for those three flights: *So sorry that there is no elevator. The lack of accommodation for persons with disabilities in this country is shocking, especially when you consider how many of us still suffer from knee injuries sustained during the Troubles.* Forewarned, I allowed myself an extra twenty minutes for the ascent, most of which I needed, clutching at the banister with one hand, at a crutch with the other (second crutch jutting peg side up, like the handle of a tennis racket, from the zipper enclosure of my backpack), hopping with my good foot, as I hauled myself up, one step at a time. Worrying the whole time that someone was going to come barreling down and send me tumbling backward like a beetle flicked off a pant leg. But no one did. In fact, there was not a student in sight, though when I reached the top landing, sweating inside my green silk and wool blend suit, it was only a few minutes before the hour. And when I pushed open the door to my classroom, I found it empty, even as the bells in the clock tower across the street had begun to chime. Shrugging off my backpack, I slipped out of my jacket, which I draped over the back of a molded plastic and chrome chair. The chair stood next to a laminate table with a whiteboard on the wall behind it—the pedagogical pulpit to a dozen or so facing desk chairs. I collapsed into the molded plastic seat. Maybe I'd gotten the time wrong, I thought, or even the day, when I'd copied it down from the course information page in my faculty portal (Malarkey promised that I would *lack for nothing*, but there is still no printer in my flat). In a little while I would begin the descent to street level, to inquire, though I wasn't exactly sure where to go, given the indeterminate location of the Queer Studies Program. In the meantime, I decided to take a short rest, leaning back against the molded plastic of my chair, which tipped and rocked slightly with the pressure. Across the room, fitted into the slope of wall, there is a casement window, which opens out over the brickwork buildings of the commercial district behind the university. Fixed to the side of one them, a billboard sign, depicting a giant bottle of beer and clock face, declares *It's Guinness Time.* I closed my eyes.

I must have slept because I dreamt of some old lover's body pushing against mine, though I don't remember whose. When I awoke, my crotch was damp (the little mouseskin merkin is gone, by the way). I would have lingered upon the sensation, but I was no longer alone. The dozen or so facing desk chairs were now filled, occupants gazing at me expectantly, with the exception of a bespectacled boy, a silky tassel of blond hair dangling over one lens, as he tapped at a laptop, and an elderly woman, wearing a floral print housedress that looked at least half a century old—like something my mother might have worn, in fact. She was bent over a large notebook and sucking at the nib of her fountain pen as she stared down at whatever she'd written (a pensioner, I assumed, tippling at higher education).

I looked back at all of them (except for the typing boy and the pen sucking old woman) looking at me. It was as if I had just paused in a speech and in a moment would resume. I crossed my legs, then raised my right index finger, I don't know why. Perhaps I thought it could serve as a sort of radio antenna, to receive the gist of whatever I was supposed to be talking about. The seconds lengthened into a minute, as I continued to sit there, mute, with my finger pointing skyward, as they all continued to stare at me, waiting to take in my next words, words I couldn't possibly utter without knowing what had preceded them. When suddenly I recalled an old teaching strategy: Would someone like to recap?

The hand of the boy who had been tapping at the laptop shot up: I've got it all here, Professor Dorn. At least I think I've got it. Shall I give it a go?

I nodded.

He was wearing an oxford cloth button down and one hand went to the collar, index finger tapping at the top button as the other adjusted his glasses, which were horn rimmed and oversized. His features were fine, almost elfin, and he looked like a model or an actor, playing the part of the serious university student. Orlando Bloom, perhaps. Peering at the screen, he cleared his throat:

Well Professor Dorn, you were explaining how identity is a fiction, as demonstrated by Professor Jacques Lacan's 'Theory of the Mirror Stage.' You said that according to Professor Lacan, the newborn child has no sense of self. It is, if I heard right, *a body in parts*. A quote unquote *spastic bundle* unable even to recognize its own limbs. He paused, looked at me for confirmation over the rims of his glasses.

Excellent, I pronounced. I uncrossed my legs and stood up, elevated by a sense of restored authority, though I refrained from stepping out into the room (which no doubt would have been my downfall). Instead, I leaned against the edge of the table, pushing up the sleeves of my peacock print shirt: Please continue.

So how does the child come to master its relationship to its body? Well it seems Professor Lacan starts with an observation about the difference between the way chimpanzees and young children relate to mirrors: the chimp loses interest once it realizes that the image is just an image, that it is *empty*, while the child seems to become fascinated.

Maybe because monkeys have better things to do, someone over near the door said. The old woman in the housedress, who was sitting in the front row, snorted. She'd set her fountain pen aside, and I saw that she'd been drawing rather than writing, though I couldn't make out the details of her sketch. I craned to see, but she was now leaning forward, her forearms on the desktop, the blousey, blossom besprigged front of her billowing over the page. The housedress was a shirtwaist style, the first several unbuttons undone, revealing the dark cleft between two great wrinkly dugs. I turned away.

Orlando Bloom continued: Professor Lacan theorizes that the child gains a sense of autonomy by identifying with an image outside itself—the mother, another child, a mirror. Quote unquote Professor Lacan, *We have only to understand the mirror stage as an identification...* So through this image of another as whole, as complete, the child comes to see itself as complete. Furthermore, Professor Lacan claims the child is predestined to do this. We can understand in what sense it is predestined through an important term he uses in the essay, which Professor Dorn has defined for us up on the board.

I looked behind me. Near the upper edge of the white vinyl surface floated the word *imago*, inked with black marker in what appeared to be my handwriting. I wondered how I'd managed the stretch, without losing my balance. Below it were three definitions, also in my handwriting:

1. An image

2. An insect in its final adult, sexually mature and usually winged state.

3. in psychoanalysis, the more or less infantile conception of the parent retained in the unconscious.

Touching his fingertip to his collar, Orlando Bloom cleared his throat: If I understood you correctly, Professor Dorn, all three definitions of imago are important. The wee child, who is unable to walk or even stand up—uses the image to gain a sense of mastery and control, whether it is the image of herself in the mirror, another wee child, or the adult she will someday become. Tis as if the image is a kind of chrysalis that transforms the wee grub into a butterfly.

He paused, pulling at the yellow tassel of his hair: I'm not sure about that last bit, which I guess is kind of my own take on things. I was going off on the insect connection.

A conspicuous yawn issued from the seat near the door. I felt my own jaw begin to unhinge, and quickly clamped it with my hand, thus affecting a posture of consideration. A girl in the back with the burnt orange hue of the tanning salon wondered if maybe it made more sense in the French?

Brilliant, I said. I tapped on my iPhone: only eleven minutes left, but that was assuming the class ended at the time indicated on the schedule I'd found in my teaching portal. Do continue.

Well as you put it, Professor Dorn, or perhaps it twas Professor Lacan, *all this comes at a price.* Because if the wee child's sense of self is formed upon another, *he is trapped in an image fundamentally alien to himself.* Or herself. As I put it meself, in my notes, *there's no there there.* Though maybe that should be there's no here here. Anyway, tis like the wee child thinks they are whole and complete, but tis only an illusion, based upon this image of wholeness that they see in the Other with a capital 'O.' Maybe I'm away in the head, but I'm thinking tis as if the wee child is a kind of hologram projected by the other. Like the butterfly is only a virtual butterfly. He paused again.

The old doodler snorted again.

I glanced over and saw that the drawing in her notebook was now uncovered, and further, that it was me: a round bodied besuited little figure (she'd drawn me with the jacket on, tight as a carapace) asleep in a chair, skinny limbs sprawled, crutches propped like spare legs against a background wall. The lines were fine, meticulous yet whimsical—suggestive of an illustration in a Victorian fairytale book. I looked away.

That's great. A virtual butterfly. More flattering than a beetle, certainly, I said. Anything more?

He shook his head: Sorry Professor Dorn, that's all I've got.

Any questions then?

So basically he's sayin' we're all bleedin' buckets? Sluts looking to be filled up by this 'Other'? the burnt orange girl scoffed.

What about blind people? Do they not have identities? asked another girl. I noted that she had gathered up her oversize handbag. Either she was getting ready to belt someone, or preparing to depart.

Blind people are the only ones with true identities of their own, surely, offered a ginger haired boy in the back. Like in advertising. If you can't see the Other's mug, you don't want it. Simple as that, really. That's why me Da would never let us have a telly or a computer. Though once we were all gone he hiked it down to the SONY Centre and now he and me mum are gawkin at screens all the day long.

The old doodler leaned back into her chair, crossing her arms over her blowsy, blossomed chest, and cocked her head at the boy. Her hair was either dyed black or a wig, improbably thick and shiny for her wizened face (at least ten years older than my own?) with its sunken ocular pips. The lips parted, and a voice emerged, a liquid, trilling brogue as fantastical as the coiffure.

The point is that you have no real self of yer own, boyo. And we Irish have always known this, have we not? For t'is in practically all the old tales, in the warp-spasm and in the Celtic phenomenon of shape-shifting, taken for granted by our ancestors the same way we now take for granted electricity or the internet. *A hawk to-day, a boar yesterday, wonderful instability.* But t'is a world view that does yer head in and that is why we've always fought each other so. If I can kill you, and live, then surely I'm me self and not you.

And now the doodler swiveled her head, with its preposterous black wave of hair, toward me.

So we don't need some obfuscating French theorist, further mucked up by an American professor, to reveal what we Irish have suspected since seamus first bashed sean—that we are essentially inessential, she concluded, elongating and swirling together vowels and consonants in a kind of steaming acoustic potion or semantic mist.

In desperation I tapped again at my phone. Thirteen minutes left, but hadn't it been eleven before? Close enough—surely it was time to surrender.

Class dismissed, I said.

With alacrity, they all rose from their seats, including the old doodler, who appeared as spry as any of them. Outside the bells began to chime again, the sound wafting through the open window, as if to provide classroom support for my decision to disband.

But the doodler remained after the others had gone, even as I didn't realize it at first. I'd told them to write their names as they were leaving on a sheet of paper (supplied by Orlando Bloom) atop the laminate table, then sunk back into my seat, pretending to check email on my iPhone (which seemed to be set at the proper time again, as far as I could tell), until I heard the door click shut. Then I'd closed my eyes: just ten minutes, I thought, to gather the strength to go. So that I felt her before I saw her. Or rather *it*. Felt it looming over me, and smelled it too, a humid billow both carnal and vegetal, a fleshy fecal muck laced with plant humus, an odor that was distantly familiar though I couldn't think why and as I opened my eyes, recollection ceased. So that all I could do now was look, my eyes wide, filling and brimming with the gray bristled flesh pouch hanging over my face, with its split of glistening mauve meat spilling forth, dazzle tipped. Dazzle tipped? I squinted, and then to be sure reached up and touched with one finger: a diamond.

A diamond, dangling from an ancient scrap of clitoris. I touched the hard little wink of stone, rubbed it between thumb and forefinger. And then poof, all gone—not just the gem, but also the clit and the twat—as she leapt away. She being the old woman, the *crone*, who'd been straddling me, and yet who was, it seemed, as agile as a cat. Through slitted eyes, I watched her hike her housedress down over her skinny loins, then fish out a pen from somewhere deep in her cleavage. As she bent over the roster to sign it, I continued to feign sleep, waiting for her to leave.

Which she finally did, but not before stooping over me one more time, one skinny arm snaking around my back, pulling me close as she whispered in my ear: sleep, little ladybug, sleep.

Then she walked out.

I listened to her feet thumping down the stairs, fading and disappearing. Had I really seen that diamond, or even its hoary vulval setting (which sans gem, no doubt mirrored my own)? And did I, after all, care? Over the course of the last year, my life had (has) gotten stranger and stranger. Stranger and ever more hurtful, beginning with that night at Conrad and Ormondo's, when I wept without restraint in front of my old enemy Marian Ferris. Yet I hadn't (haven't) cried since. Not even tears of rage. FYI Madmaeve: even now, as I write this, my eyes are dry as a bone.

I wasn't yet ready to descend, and after a while I drifted off again. This time the lover in my dream was someone specific: Kevin. Only there was no body to be seen, just a face in a cave, floating white like a moon or a mushroom cap in the darkness. There was no body to be seen, but I was sure one was there. Or most of a body, missing leg, or rather foot and calf (the one leg being a stump that ended at the knee) notwithstanding, and in my dream I ached for it. Kevin always claimed that he could still feel the missing parts and sometimes would wake in the middle of the night, doubled up in pain, as if the hotel bar blast was lacerating him all over again. Likewise in my dream I pulsed for the feel of those phantom limbs tangled with my own, throbbed as hard or harder for Kevin's missing body as I ever had for the real one, pulsed and throbbed, pulsed and throbbed... When suddenly flesh smacked against flesh, only from every side, an all encompassing carnal slap from a source I could not see. I woke up.

My skin still tingled, but unlike before, I felt no lingering desire, only the prickle of mortification. The prickle of mortification and then, suddenly, a white-hot flare of wrath. There is no way out, I thought. No way out, as fury filled my chest, rose up in my throat. I opened my mouth to scream, but no sound emerged. No sound at all. And certainly no tears—as mentioned above, the time for those had passed. Like there was no vent, no escape from the stifling shell of self (*sleep little ladybug, sleep*), not anymore.

But had there ever been? For twenty years, as an associate professor of Gender Studies, teaching the anti-essentialism of theorists like Jacques Lacan, not to mention Judith Butler (whom, Madmaeve, I believe you recently blogged was your "fave"), to one crop of graduate students after another (which always yielded a new lover or two, at least for the first fifteen years or so), I'd fucked my brains out. And hadn't they always come back? Whether they were (in)essentially mine, or some (m)other's (definitely not Margaret's, I'm sure of that. Though I'll admit I was a bit of a Daddy's girl), wasn't the neural circuit invariably the same? Sandra Dorn Sandra Dorn Sandra Dorn like a hedge of thorn, the rosy ring of a mind that had gone nowhere despite my parting promise, when I left Kevin's baby behind, that I was finally going to make something more of myself—no more drinking and drugging, fighting and fucking. Well not no more fucking, but no more flailing about in the sand pit of Sandra-hood, dabbling at mud pies and silt cakes (*there's a difference woman, between raw and half-baked*). Finally, I promised myself, I'd go back to school, drive my intellect beyond the limits of ego, lose myself in the study of some movement or current of thought that carries the self beyond the self, like sex but without the inevitable carnal recoil.

Somewhere down below, perhaps as far down as street level, a door slammed. I couldn't tell if someone was exiting the building or entering, but either way, it was time to go back down. I didn't want to be caught in the upward rush of whatever class followed my own.

Using the table for support, I stood up. A breeze was blowing in through the casement window and I could hear a bird cooing out under the eves, a pigeon or maybe a dove. I picked up the attendance list to put it away in my backpack. The last name was illegible, but for a sweeping "M," presiding over the ensuing scrawl. *Sleep little ladybug, sleep.*

I slid my arms into my jacket, then buttoned it. Was the fit really as snug as depicted in the old doodler's drawing? I skimmed my hand down over my abdomen—felt the silk wool fabric stretched tight, straining at the brass buttons. It was as if I was pregnant again, the suit material substituting for the tautened skin of gravity. I unbuttoned the jacket, shrugging it off with the intention of folding it away in my backpack when a folded square of paper fell out of the pocket. I bent down to retrieve it.

The stock was thick—a sheet of drawing paper from M's sketchbook, I guessed. Or a portion of one, since the folded square was too small to be composed of an entire page. Perhaps she'd done a cameo, a close-up of my sleeping face, eyes closed and mouth agape. Painstakingly precise, but without a breath of life, so that you wouldn't be able to tell if I was alive or dead. The open window delivered a sudden chill and I shivered in my peacock print shirt. I decided to put the jacket back on—it would be easier to do it up here than down at street level, teetering on crutches. Since there was no trash basket in the room, I restored the folded square to the pocket. I'd dispose of it at home.

The climb down was even more arduous than the ascent. White knuckling the bannister with one hand, I gripped a crutch with the other, planting the tip a step at a time, as I swung my good leg, the left, forward. By the time I reached the first landing, my quadriceps were quivering from the effort. I rested for a moment, peering down over the railing to the bottom of the stairwell, which was closed off by a wooden door. At any moment the first head would break through, followed by the student body, a barreling mass of arms and legs and backpacks and computer bags. I could wait for the crush, or I could attempt to avoid it by at least getting to the next level, where earlier I'd noticed a sign for a study lounge. I decided to plunge ahead.

Which I did, literally, seconds later, my left leg giving way on the second step, pitching me forward into a tumble which must have involved a cascade of bumps, thumps and thwacks, and surely, with the final impact against the door, if not prior, splinters and cracks, but I can't say for sure because I have no memory of anything beyond the precipitating collapse of my limb.

When I came to, the door was open and I was sprawled on my stomach with my legs behind me in the stairwell, my upper body resting in the landing just above the ground floor so that I could see through the railings to the vestibule below. I propped myself up on one elbow, and looked back at my legs. They looked okay—nothing unnatural in their angles. Not only that, but the dull throb of pain in the thigh of the bad leg, my right, the persistent ache that had become part of my somatic status quo, was gone. Maybe I was paralyzed. I twisted my torso, craning to get a better look and realized as I did so that I'd just lifted my right thigh. I bent the knee, raised it up, lowered it down, up again in a scissor kick, rotated it in a circle. It was fine, and likewise with the other as I pulled myself first up on my knees, and then stood without the assistance of crutches, for the first time in months. In the bottom panel of the door, on the stairwell side, there was a big crack in the wood. I ran my hands up and down my arms and legs, palmed the contours of my hips, probed the surface of my skull for corresponding contusions, but found nothing. I found nothing even as I felt my skin warming to my own touch, thrilling beneath my fingers as if they belonged to some electrifying new lover. I felt great. Like I was thirty again, with bounce in my legs and brio in my cunt.

I left my crutches for the taking, leaning against the wall outside the study lounge. Perhaps someone had sprained an ankle, cavorting on the cricket field or the dance floor. Then I sauntered down the stairs, reaching the front door just as the throng of students I'd been dreading came pressing in. Only there was no crush, or rather, it didn't crush me. Instead, I felt enlarged, expanded, as if it were 1987 and I was raving on ecstasy, swimming in a sweaty warehouse sea of strangers. I floated through as if flesh and bone and backpacks had dissolved into soup or amniotic fluid but when the tide had finally passed and I was standing outside on the sidewalk alone, I was not marooned.

Rather, I was delivered. Yes, delivered. I stood on the empty pavement, chin lifted and fists on my hips, and surveyed the scene, like a sailor with unlimited shore leave and a shucking knife in his pocket. It was beautiful, not raining for once, the waning light clear. Parked cars lined both sides of the street, metal shells gleaming nacreous shades of blue and red and gray. I could smell the rank autumnal remains of the row house gardens behind me, and drifting in from the Malone road beyond, the odor of fish frying, scales crisping in oil. In a little while I'd go find the pub that was serving it. Batter fried haddock, tap beer and a rockapaddy band. Boozy sentiment and sodality, I'd slurp it all up. And after, I'd walk home alone, drinking the night air as a chaser. Delivered, I understood that the world was mine. And nothing more. It was like waking up from a bad dream. Maybe, I thought, that's all any of it—the beetles, the hare episode, the bad leg—had been. A bad dream (*sleep little Ladybug, sleep*), a fantasy of persecution, a psychosomatic fabrication of extrinsic pursuit.

I reached into my jacket pocket for my cigarettes. And that's when I felt the little square of paper. I fiddled with it, pressed the pad of my index finger against one pointy corner. It would only be a drawing, however cruel and belittling, and now that I was delivered, I understood that the choice to be piqued was mine alone. I pulled the square out, unfolded it, and discovered there was in fact no drawing, just printed-out words, a summons of sorts, in a sans serif font:

Join the Party.
A black taxi cab will pick ye up outside yer apartment building, at 11:45 pm sharp this Saturday night.
M

That was two days ago, Madmaeve. In less than 24 hours my "black taxi cab" is due to arrive. Back in 1978, when I first moved to Belfast with Kevin, well before you were even born, black cabs were how we got around town since the city bus drivers refused to navigate the various factional snakepits, not to mention the bomb craters. Now of course the black cab is the iconic vehicle of a thriving industry in politico-tourism, and both Paddy and Paul are raking in the pounds driving foreign rubberneckers through the old bullet pocked "peace lines." So I'm guessing that my ride is to be taken tongue in cheek (with care not to bite it off going over the potholes), and that when I reach my destination, wherever it may be, the command to *join the party* (I'm envisioning some polished pub in the city centre, with a good, ecumenical whiskey list) will not be compulsory. Though as the guest "prof," I may be pressed for a round or two.

On the other hand, I did hear that City Cemetery bomb go off last night, though it sounded far away and I couldn't identify the locale. You must have heard it, too. According to those two blow-outs I heard earlier, discussing the blast over their frappes, it was intended for the police. No one was hurt, but a wee Filipino family driving by had been treated for shock. *I wonder if they'll go back to their own country now*, one of the blow-outs had said. Oh Belfast is still a nasty place, as you've written yourself, Madmaeve, in many a post: racist and sexist as well as incorrigibly sectarian (what was that article you linked the other day from the *Guardian*? Something about how the schools are still 90 per cent segregated and how the majortity of Ulster's children grow up never having a serious conversation with the other tribe?). So I'm not entirely discounting the possibility that something "real," something extrinsic, could happen to me tomorrow night. No doubt there are still Killeens about and though a self-absorbed lot (I don't think any of them ever even bothered to learn my "maiden" name), who surely wouldn't recognize me on the street at this point anyway (nor I them), you never know. An abduction, ala Jean McConville or Lisa Dorrian—I suppose it could happen. A bullet in the back of the head, a trip in the boot, a dump in the dunes or even a bog—why not? The subject's death (c'était moi, s'il vous plaît) substantiated by a paragraph in the local news: The body of an unidentified female, age sixty five to seventy, was discovered by

a jogger
strand.
tim ap-
have suf-
ballistic
w o u n d
head. A
investi-
is under-
subject's
substan-
a few days
cades (it
years to
r e m a i n s
McCon-
maybe,
discrete-
peat,
No
what,
ready, for
ever, to
er my ride
Perhaps it
you.

Curbside, it sits.
Like a shiny black gourd.
Like an enormous gintry beetle,
Glittered with drizzle.

Yer hoping it will just fly away,
When the passenger door unfolds.
There is only the runnel of gutter to cross:
A teeny Sweeney leap.

The driver grunts: *Hiya.*
Ye sink back, close yer eyes.
Tis an automotive lull,
Quiet as gestation.

Tires roll over asphalt, the engine hums,
A late night radio voice solicitously drones:
Are you living with a long-term condition?
We are here to help.

Ye sleep and the city unravels,
Lights straggling,
fields spreading like legs.
Yer gob gapes and moans.

Up ahead, two wee flares in the mizzle:
Something alive paused over something dead,
Alive bolts and a wheel thumps over dead.
The driver guns it.

on the
The vic-
pears to
fered a
t r a u m a
to the
p o l i c e
g a t i o n
way. The
d e a t h
tiated in
or de-
took 30
find the
of Jean
ville) or
given the
ness of
never.
m a t t e r
I am
w h e r -
whomev-
takes me.
will be to

The dark is lifting,
Broken yolks of whin splatter gray green hills.
The black taxi turns off the main road
Into a canal of hedges.

Pavement yields to dirt and pebbles,
Spitting and dinging and pocking.
Yer eyes slit and yer toes
Squirm inside yer shoes.

A palm cups yer elbow, guiding ye up and out:
We are here to help.
Inside yer trousers,
A trickle of piss slides down yer thigh.

Somewhere *the ack-ack of the corncrake,*
The peewit of the plover: a **senseless soundstripe.**
The smell of cow dung in the wind,
Meadow grasses and sweet hay turned to shite.

A farm lies just beyond the rise.
But there's nobody there but us chickens
And the cattle never tattle.
The driver trots ye down the slope.

Midges burlap yer head and
Dew weights yer cuffs then swamp water
As grass becomes quagmire,
Seeping and farting beneath yer feet.

A turf spade hidden under bracken.
Finders keepers, **the driver snickers,**
And passes it to ye.
Ye lift and ye thrust, but there is no split.

No *soft lips* **in the growth,**
No *tawny rut* **no** *wettish shaft.*
Ye collapse.
The spade or a stroke. Take yer pick.

The ground slips and slops and sinks
Like a water bed or a bad excuse.
Shivers and heaves and shakes
But it does not give.

It does not give even as the bog
slimes yer body
like a new placenta
All but yer sorry fucking head.

Get up, the driver says.
The sun slices yer sclera and the sky is carving
Itself out into a hard blue bowl.
The muck on yer skin begins to bake.

But at the edges, something is beginning
To fissure and fracture,
To crack like an egg or a chrysalis
Or a skull.

We are here to help.

On two legs, on four, on six, on eight
And none at all.
Dressed in skin, feathers, fur, horns, bristles,
Scales, membranes and chitin

We are here to help.

Dancing, prancing, swooping and diving, scampering,
scuttling, scooting, creeping and slithering,

We are here to help.

Singing, chanting, hooting, mewling, barking, cawing,
Screeching, buzzing, hissing and humming,

We are here to help.

With hands and feet, fingers and toes, paws and claws,
Feelers and fronds,
With mouths, lips, tongues, noses, beaks, proboscises,
Pizzles, spurs and dainty denticles

We are here to help.

Licking, sucking, nuzzling, kneading, slurping, sapping,
Poking, prodding, pricking, jabbing, stabbing,
Boring and tunneling

Through grimaces and winces, shudders and shivers,
Jerks and judders, wracks and wrenches, spasms,
Throes, propulsions and even screams

We are here to whelp.

Plumbing cavities, suffusing tissues, hollowing bones,
Snaking veins, flushing corpuscles, scattering synapses,
Ravaging and savaging—

We
will
rout
you
out

ELISABETH SHEFFIELD is the author of four novels, *Ire Land (A Faery Tale)*, published by Spuyten Duyvil (2021), *Helen Keller Really Lived* (FC2 2014), *Fort Da: A Report* (FC2 2009), and *Gone* (FC2 2003), as well as a critical book on James Joyce. A National Endowment of the Arts Award for Literature Fellow in 2012, Elisabeth Sheffield has also been awarded two Fulbrights, in Kiel, Germany (1999-2000), and in Belfast, Northern Ireland (2014), and a writing residency at the Hanse Institute for Advanced Study in Bremen, Germany (2016-2017). She teaches in the Creative Writing program at the University of Colorado at Boulder, and lives in Boulder and upstate NY with the writer Jeffrey DeShell, two boys, two cats and a shiba inu. https://www.elisabethsheffield.com

Made in the USA
Las Vegas, NV
22 December 2022

63820664R00121